Enjoy!

T Z Fischer

The Cozies
The Legend of Operation Moonlight

by T.L. Fischer

with illustrations by Kory Fluckiger

PRINTED IN THE USA

The Cozies: The Legend of Operation Moonlight / T.L. Fischer — First Print Edition

ISBN: 978-1-94768-201-6 (print)

ISBN: 978-1-94768-200-9 (ebook)

Published in the United States of America

The nursery figments' parlor rests

inside the window seat,

behind dark walnut panels and

small children's swinging feet.

Contents

PROLOGUE

A Birth of Sorts

(an essay by the guest speaker, reprinted with permission)

Augie could not sleep. He did not *want* to sleep.
The adventures of the day whirled in his little head like streamers fluttering 'round a maypole. He'd gone to the Fair! It was a day he would never forget, with music and laughter dancing together arm-in-arm . . . pretty ladies holding parasols weightless as dandelion seeds . . . and dashing gentlemen—one in an unforgettable, emerald-green, cutaway coat.

A long-nosed man with a white face lurched by on stilts. A fat lady with painted eyes tried to give Augie a hug. A strong man stared at him over curling mustaches. Augie looked away, but couldn't help looking back. The man surprised him with a big grin, and everyone laughed.

And the animals! Beasts big as a room that snorted and pawed the straw. Augie tightened his grip on Momma's hand. He preferred the rabbits, especially those with long flowing ears that drooped from the sides of shy, furry faces. Augie held one, with Momma's help—a black one with a twitching nose.

Augie loved that bunny. He decided he would take it home. They would curl up together like the bunnies in their pen.

Momma and Poppa said no. Saying goodbye to the bunny with the floppy ears was hard for Augie. So he threw a fit, briefly, and napped in Poppa's arms.

But that night, back at home in his own bed, Augie refused to surrender. He fought to stay awake so he could relive the day's adventures over and over again.

Eventually, though, the evening air cooled. Damp curls on his forehead dried and curled tighter. Augie started slipping off to sleep. Real memories mingled with imagined. The maypole streamers of Augie's dreamy thoughts pulled loose, twirling up and away on a swirling breeze.

Nearby, the nursery curtains stirred. The Moon's bright-beaming face peeked through.

The last thing Augie saw, or perhaps the first thing he dreamed, was a tiny gentleman in an emerald-green cutaway coat, standing in the bluish moonlight beside his pillow. A tiny gentleman whose head was that of a black, floppy-eared rabbit.

PART ONE

Two First Tuesdays of the Month

1

Welcome

(Jungfrau Room, October 13, 1927, 9:00 a.m.)

Welcome, Ladies and Gentlemen. My name is Thursby, and I have been asked to speak to you about the importance of imagination in human affairs. As you may have guessed, imagination is a subject with which I am personally familiar.

(The speaker pauses for laughter to subside.)

No, your eyes do not deceive you. But let me describe myself for those who will study these talks later in transcript form. For the sake of accuracy, I will refrain from my usual modesty—much as it pains me to sing my own praises.

Although just under five inches tall, I am dressed in a green cutaway coat, a blue waistcoat, a white shirt and neckcloth, and charcoal-gray trousers. Eternally elegant, though I grant you, not so fashionable now as in a past century.

I stand upright with a youthful and athletic physique. And yet—and some consider this my most distinctive feature—my head is that of a floppy-eared rabbit. An English lop rabbit, as you may have deduced from my accent. Not just any English lop, obviously, but one covered with soft, black fur of the most exquisite nature.

(The speaker smooths his ears, then turns his head to display his appearance.)

Those of you in the back might think that I am wearing gloves—a common error, as my fur extends even over my otherwise humanish hands. I wear no shoes due to the functional size of my rabbity feet.

(One foot is extended from behind the podium.)

There again, my black fur completes the ensemble.

As you've no doubt surmised, I am what is commonly called a figment of the imagination. Now, generally speaking, figments do not inhabit this so-called real world. We are beings of the world of dreams. The *Traumwelt. Le monde des rêves.*

Please note that I am appearing here by special arrangement. The legal details are set forth in the lecture-series brochure.

There are exceptions. My colleagues and I, for example, are nursery figments—or *Cozies* as we are called in dreams where English is spoken. As such, we are visible to small children. And cats, of course, and most dogs.

In fact, it is in the imaginations of children that my kind originate. Whether we come into this world by coincidence or design is a matter of debate. But the physics have been established; to wit: Nursery figments are nudged into the physical world when moonlight enters a home and touches a child's happy dreams.

This explains why our existence here is so closely tied to that most popular of celestial orbs—the Moon.

(The speaker nods to his assistant, who turns back the flip-chart title page to reveal Exhibit #1: "Primary Source of Moonlight.")

For it is only when bathed by moonlight that Cozies become visible to adult humans. Only by moonlight do we gain full access to this world. Complex, I know, but I will explain the scientific details more as we proceed.

We will now pause briefly to allow any latecomers to find their seats. Also, I've been asked to announce that the seminar *Green Dreams: Absinthe in Victorian England* is next door in the Matterhorn Room. By the bewildered expression on some faces, it appears that a few of you may've wandered into the wrong conference room.

Before we break, let me say that this talk will not rely on my published treatises. Those documents are for sale in the lobby, past the refreshment table. Instead I will share a tale from my own long experience: a story of simple pleasures and high-flying adventure . . . old friends and new enemies . . . bright ideas and dark shadows.

A story of imagination.

Please limit the break to no more than ten minutes.

*　　*　　*

2

The First Tuesday of the Month

If you'll please take your seats, Ladies and Gentlemen. Thank you.

(The speaker pauses to allow the chatter to die down.)

My tale unfolds in a grand house in the country on a Tuesday afternoon. Upstairs at the end of the long hallway was the nursery, which overlooked the garden. One-year-old Bingo, whose real name was Benjamin, napped peacefully in his crib.

Mother—that is to say, Bingo's mother—had slept in the same crib when she was a baby. Ah, many a night had I spent sitting on the crib rail, singing lullabies to her. Now she was all grown up, resting in a chair beside her own child. To me, though, she was still that pretty little girl with long, dark eyelashes.

With no sound in the nursery but the rain on the bay windows, Mother had fallen asleep in her chair beside the crib.

For the household Cozies, though, it was not simply a lazy, rainy day in the nursery.

This was the first Tuesday of the month—time for Musetta's monthly theatrical presentation. She was scheduled to perform *Pining Maiden, Part III.* The playbills described this as Musetta's greatest work ever.

Admittedly, there were those who suspected that an "I" had simply been added to the playbills for *Pining Maiden, Part II.* Nevertheless, we were filled with anticipation as we gathered in our usual places. Gubbins, Rumple, and I took seats on the leaf-and-vine designs of the window-seat cushion.

"Tik-whir-whir, tik-tik, tik-tik-tik, tik-tik-tik-tik— *Pa-ding!*—" said Gubbins. Gubbins speaks mainly in clicking and whirring sounds, you see, with the odd chimes, bells, and whistles thrown in. Actually, this can be exhausting to listen to. So I occasionally interrupt once the basic idea is out.

"Quite so," I put in, knowing that *Pa-ding!* was Gubbins' pet mouse. The rest of us mimicked the chime by calling her Pudding. "Still, we couldn't have Pudding out in broad daylight, could we?"

While nursery figments are invisible to adults, mice are not. Also, to be blunt, Cozies are far more hygienic than mice. Far more.

"—tik-tik-tik-tik, tik, tik-whir-tik, tik!" finished Gubbins.

Gubbins is as hard to describe as he is to listen to. You could say he resembles what might happen if two pocket watches collided and the bits and pieces came down in the shape of a little person about my size—gears, sprockets, springs, and so forth.

Musetta waved at us from the far end of the window seat. I nodded. The diva crossed regally toward us.

"Girls!" I whispered to the Twins, Gracie and Ruby. They stopped bouncing on the big burgundy pillow and looked at me, then at each other, with wide-eyed, bemused expressions. "Musetta is about to begin."

Round-faced girls no bigger than a man's thumb, each with pretty but ineffectual little wings, each twin is a mirror image of the other, right down to their pink tutus and white-blond curls. Using first initials as reminders, we had decided that whichever twin was on the right would be Ruby, with Gracie on the left. *En français*, of course, to be on the left is to be *à gauche*, with a "g."

The Twins snuck in one last bounce, then plopped down on the pillow embroidery of a maharajah riding an elephant.

Musetta walked over to Rumple, who sat near the window. She stepped right up his translucent, baby-blue body to the top of his head. With a shove off of one foot, Musetta was on the window sill.

Rumple looked around, doubly confused by what someone might have been doing climbing on him and the sudden appearance of Musetta on the sill. He made no comment, of course, because Rumple does not speak. Nor are we certain that he actually thinks. But he does feel, bless his heart, and that's what counts most.

The thing is, Rumple was something of a nursery-figment preemie. He was also the most recent addition to our family of figments. One night when Bingo was little more than a newborn babe, gurgling and grinning and gazing up at nothing—nothing visible, that is—a moonbeam chanced in and POOF! There was Rumple, round and softish and, to put it bluntly, sort of half-formed.

Baby Bingo may have been imagining the maharajah's elephant on the big burgundy pillow, for there is something elephantine to Rumple. He's nearly as big as the rest of us put together. His ears, though, are smallish, and his nose is more like that of a tapir than an elephant.

All our attention focused on Musetta. The rain-streaked window provided a perfect backdrop. Specks of raindrop-befuddled light blended shades of gray with the verdant hues of tree tops in the garden—an effect quite like an Impressionist painting. Cozies are naturally partial to Impressionist art. The blurs of light and color are much like our view of the real world from the world of dreams.

Ah, Musetta! *Quelle beauté!* Kohl-eyed, with an aquiline nose, she radiates mystery, elegance, charm. Of course, her dramatic looks might not suit everyone. The imaginings of a toddler a long, long time ago might not match later ideals of beauty any more than a lop-eared rabbit . . . Never mind, that's not a good example. Everyone loves a lop-eared rabbit.

Musetta's height adds to her willowy appearance. She stands at least a head taller than yours truly.

(lifts floppy ears upright to demonstrate referenced height)

Her high-waisted dress shines a plum-purple nearly black. One might describe the dress as slinky if it didn't cover her from the top of her fair shoulders to her tiny feet. Her gloves continue up to her elbows. On her head she sports a velvet wrap. At her forehead, from behind an amethyst broach, a golden plume fans upward. Dark curls frame her alabaster face.

Musetta breathed in deeply, turned her head to one side, and closed her eyes. The performance was about to begin.

★   ★   ★

3

Dramaticus Interruptus

Suddenly . . .

(dramatic pause)

. . . an interruption.

"Ma'am, excuse me," said Bridie, the family's red-haired, rosy-cheeked housekeeper. Bridie touched Mother's shoulder to rouse her. "Ma'am. The lady's here about the nanny position."

The Twins popped up and started jumping up and down. Their little wings fluttered with excitement.

"The new nanny!" squealed Gracie.

"Let's go see her! Let's go see her!" cried Ruby.

"Whirrrrr!" joined Gubbins, with his shorthand, such as it is, for "whir-tik-whir-whirrrrr." All that to simply say *Yes*.

Rumple started clapping, not uncommon at times of general commotion.

Musetta slumped her shoulders as if to say, You've got to be kidding. All the same, her curiosity equaled the rest of ours.

"Shall we take the Dinmont?" she suggested.

"The Dinmont—yayyyy!" shouted the Twins.

Musetta sprang off of the sill and took a step off of Rumple to join us on the cushion. Looking up at the now-empty window sill, Rumple applauded.

Ruby and Gracie bounced off of the big burgundy pillow and ran to the window seat's edge. "DAN-DEEEEEE!" they screeched in unison. Bingo, who had started to fuss on being lifted from the crib, laughed and pointed over Mother's shoulder in our direction. The Twins clapped their chubby hands over their mouths and shared a delighted giggle at the outrageous sound they'd made.

"For goodness' sake, girls," said Musetta, "Dandie's right there." The family dog, a Dandie Dinmont terrier, had been lying at Mother's feet. Yes, a Dandie Dinmont named Dandie. I assure you, 'twasn't a Cozy named him.

With a few subtle kissy sounds, Musetta caught the dog's attention just as Mother, with Bingo in arms, left the nursery. Dandie trotted over to the alcove and pulled up alongside the window seat. Ears back, tail wagging, he looked adoringly and adorably up at Musetta.

"What a good doggy," cooed Musetta. "Yes you are!"

Problem was, another household pet watched this—jealously. Pudding the mouse had been waiting patiently inside our parlor entrance along the baseboard. The Dinmont's activity, though, proved too much.

Baring her tiny-but-sharp rodent teeth, Pudding launched from the parlor entrance, barking. I use the term bark loosely. In truth, it sounded more like a cross between a squeak and a miniature sneeze. Yes, Pudding wore a collar decorated with little paw prints, but she was really just a house mouse.

Dandie, however, imagined Pudding to be a threat, and that was enough. Tail between his legs, sneeze-squeeking rodent at his heels, Dandie ran circles in the bay-window alcove. Then, after some desperate slipping of paws on the hardwood, he sprinted out for wider circles around the crib.

Gubbins chimed "Pa-ding!" Musetta and I vociferated, and Gracie and Ruby launched straight into a panic, screaming and running back and forth along the window-seat edge. Rumple applauded.

Within seconds Pudding cornered Dandie in the nook between the wardrobe and the toy chest. The hound scrunched his long, low back so high he looked like a frightened cat. Pudding, now growling a tiny mouse-growl, padded toward her prey.

Suddenly something clicked for them both. Dandie cocked his head to one side. Pudding froze and—if you'll permit a bit of anthropomorphizing—grimaced. We all fell silent.

Pudding stretched one hind leg ever so slightly back toward the alcove . . . slowly, slowly, and . . . ran with Dandie right at her heels. From the window seat, we chimed and shouted and panicked all over again in reverse, shouting "Dandie, no!" and "Run, Pudding!"

Ahead by no more than the length of her tail—which, fortunately, was wrapped tightly under her belly as she ran—Pudding shot back inside the window seat through our narrow entrance in the baseboard. Dandie snarfled at the entrance, winding up with an indignant harrumph.

Thankfully, this episode did not put an end to Pudding's canine delusions. Her misplaced instincts would play a vital role on a day not far off.

More on that later in this allocution.

*   *   *

4

Once a Rascal

The fundamental mission of Cozies is to keep children contented at night. As imaginary beings, of course, our resources are limited. Nevertheless, we do our best. We sing to our young charges, we tell them stories, we dance and act silly and otherwise entertain them. Above all, we help by simply being with them.

A peaceful atmosphere is especially important for babies— Exhibit Two, if you please—

(Flip-chart Exhibit #2: "Baby at Night")

EXHIBIT #2

and for very small children. Perhaps that is why Cozies prefer, well . . . being cozy.

Not that we don't enjoy excitement. But we prefer to plan and partake of our little adventures in the warmth of our own home. We will soon discuss another kind of excitement—the kind enjoyed only after everything has, hopefully, turned out all right.

The Dandie-Pudding Incident had provided quite enough excitement for me for one day. I decided to visit Great-grandfather—that is to say, Bingo's great-grandfather—instead of joining the expedition to the ground floor.

My fellow Cozies protested against my decision. As Musetta said while signaling Dandie to hold still, "Suit yourself." Hm. In retrospect, perhaps the protest was mainly in their disappointed expressions.

In any event, I stood back as Musetta directed the others to the window-seat edge. "Everyone line up," she instructed. "Aaaand *jump!*"

"Weeeeeeeeeeee!" went the Twins as they and Gubbins and Musetta jumped off of the window seat and onto Dandie's conveniently long back. The Twins nestled into the fluffy tuft that crowned the hound's head.

Gubbins' eyes adjusted to look back up at the window seat. His right eye, you see, telescopes in and out to focus. His left eye, on the other hand, is like a watch spring that coils and expands as needed. *Why?* you might ask of Gubbins' unusual visual widgets. Ah, but who could say? As humans are said to be fifty percent water, Cozies are at least half whimsy.

"Tik-whir-tik," began Gubbins, but he also simply pointed, saving us the wait for a whole four-letter word. I mean the four-letter word *Look*, by the way.

"Thursby," Musetta said from her seat at Dandie's shoulder blades, "help Rumple, 'kay? He must've jumped up but not forward again."

Rumple was sitting near the window-seat edge, looking around himself as if wondering why there was no Dinmont there. I gave him a nudge to send him over and onto Dandie's hindquarters.

"Go get Momma!" Musetta urged Dandie. "Go get Momma!" With that, the Dinmont set off at a healthy trot.

We'll catch up with the Cozies à la Dinmont in a moment. Right now I want to introduce you to a dear friend.

First, though, you may have noticed that I use a folded umbrella as a pointing device. An umbrella, I've found, is an indispensable tool for the gentleman Cozy. One can use it to direct others' attention . . .

(points at flip chart)

. . . to lean on . . .

(leans)

or simply as a dashing fashion accessory.

(strikes dashing pose)

Most importantly, an umbrella acts as a conveyance—for short drops, at least. Far too uncontrolled for riding on the wind, as I discovered when Mother was a little girl. You see, she had a penchant for flying kites—

But I digress.

After the others left, I popped open my umbrella and stepped off of the window seat for a quick drop in elevation.

After touching down, I smoothed my ears. First things first, *n'est-ce pas?* As they say: *Nothing's so fine as floppy ears, but jumbled messes just bring jeers.* Then I strolled across the nursery floor and out to the rich colors and intricate patterns of the runner in the long hallway.

Musetta's laughter, the Twins' giggling, and Gubbins' cuckoo-clock chimes—his way of laughing—reached me all the way from the stairhall. A bouncy Dinmont-ride down a curving staircase is enough to make anyone chortle!

Great-grandfather's door stood open. Bridie, the housekeeper, was attending to him.

"Oh, Athair Críonna," said Bridie, using her Gaelic term of endearment for the old fellow, "I canna tell you how excited I am! I've not seen my niece since she was but a wee babe."

Great-grandfather's only response was a low grunt. He seldom spoke anymore. Words were harder for him to form, but mostly he just didn't have the interest in it. He simply sat in his wooden wheelchair, facing the rain-streaked window. His head listed to one side.

Bridie insisted on talking to Great-grandfather, even if he didn't seem to care.

Straightening the woolen blanket that covered the old fellow's lap, Bridie added, "The sun was shinin' the mornin' she left, here if not there, so her journey's sure to be fair."

She stepped back and looked at Great-grandfather. She followed his gaze out the window to make sure he had a view. "There, now, looks like you're settled."

"Yes, yes," he muttered from the right side of his mouth. "Go on, now, girl. Leave me be."

"Well, I'll check back in a bit."

After Bridie left, I walked over beside the wheelchair. Seeing the old fellow's face broke my little figment heart. No, it was more what I did *not* see: curiosity, laughter, courage. Those qualities had shone in his face from the time he was a tiny rascal with sandy ringlets, through his years as a strapping young man, and right up to his later years.

Now . . . not.

Only a year or so before, Great-grandfather had still been blessed with good health. Early each morning he would walk briskly around the estate. On Sundays, he would drive separately from the rest of the family in his tilbury carriage, pulled by Nellie, his horse. After church, they enjoyed jaunts in the countryside.

Not long after Bingo was born, Great-grandfather suffered an attack of apoplexy. The years, to paraphrase Horace, had finally robbed him of his joy.

I climbed the wheelchair spokes and up onto his bony right arm. I paused to study his face for a moment.

As a youth, his hazel eyes had smoldered like the warmth in his heart. In his smile, kindness had tempered mischief. In his words, charm had softened boldness.

All I could see in his face now was . . . worry, perhaps? Fear? Nothing happy, in any case.

Grabbing handfuls of sweater, I continued up to Great-grandfather's shoulder. Only thin white wisps of hair remained. His skin resembled the skin of his youth about as much as a raisin resembles a grape. But inside him, I knew, was the little boy whose childhood whimsy had created me long ago.

I stroked his wisps of hair and kissed him on the cheek. Then I took a seat on his shoulder. Together we watched the rain.

★   ★   ★

5

A Fairly Typical Cozy Evening

(The speaker has taken a moment to compose himself and daub his eyes with a royal-blue hand-kerchief. He returns to the podium.)

"Thurs-beeeeee!" shouted the Twins when I returned to the parlor. By parlor, I mean the Cozies' abode inside the nursery window seat, not Mother and Father's drawing room, which was off the stairhall on the ground floor, and considerably larger.

"We hate her!" declared Gracie.

"The new nanny," clarified Ruby.

"Hate?" I said. "That's not a nice word—especially for cosies*!"

(*Transcriptionist Note: Where the speaker quotes himself, spelling follows the British mode. As the speaker points out ad nauseam often, he is a Cozy with attributes of an English lop rabbit.)

Gracie shrugged one shoulder and an eyebrow in an impression of Musetta that wasn't half bad. I considered suggesting impressions rather than singing for the Twins' next talent show. The inevitable impression of myself put me off the idea.

The Twins went back to playing with Rumple, who sat in his usual spot on the large oval rug. Truth is, Rumple was more of an oversized toy for the girls than a playmate. Still, he seemed to enjoy being a part of their games.

At the moment, the Twins were entertaining each other by "rumpling" themselves. They would stand near Rumple on opposite sides and circle him. Through his translucent body, their images warped in weird ways—like seeing oneself in a fun-house mirror.

Gracie crossed her bright-blue eyes, puffed out her cheeks, and pressed her face against Rumple's back. On the other side, a magnified and distorted copy of Gracie's face popped into Rumple's belly. This sent Ruby into a giggle fit, which sent Gracie into a giggle fit, which all inspired a fit of squeak-barking from Pudding over by Gubbins at his drafting table.

Rumple, of course, applauded.

While this was going on, Musetta practiced dramatic poses by the fireplace.

"What's this about the new nanny?" I asked loudly, what with all the giggling and squeak-barking.

"The woman hardly said two words," said Musetta, carefully placing one gloved, long-fingered hand on the mantle. "But something about her irked me."

"An irking woman—imagine! Now I wish I'd seen her myself. Cosies seldom respond to people like this."

With one hand on the mantle, Musetta turned the other way and brought the back of her free hand to her forehead. To allow the dramatic arts to percolate, I held my tongue and dropped into one of three fireside armchairs.

Musetta paused for a moment in thought. Then she gripped the mantle more tightly and adjusted her feet. As usual, she cut an impressive figure. Firelight flickered as plum highlights along the side of her gown.

With the back of one hand at her forehead again, she breathed in deeply. "Oh-me," she sighed. In every sense, she captured the timbre of one who pines.

Freezing that way, she looked at me sidelong. "Well?" she asked.

"By George, you've got it, Musetta. You've absolutely pegged it."

"Thanks. There's more pining in *Part III* than in *I* and *II* combined."

Goodness, I thought, that's a lot of pining. But Musetta was the playwright, so I simply gave an impressed nod while smoothing my whiskers. Not that my whiskers needed smoothing. As you see, they extend out straight as pipe cleaners.

Musetta left off her rehearsal and came around behind my armchair. She held out a gloved hand on each side of my head.

"Ears," she demanded.

"Oh, Musetta, I'm not sure I'm up to *Lop-Ear Theatre* tonight— too perturbed by this new-nanny whatsit."

"Ears."

Reluctantly, I leaned forward to unpin the silky accessories from between my back and the armchair. I say reluctantly because Musetta sometimes entertains the Twins using my ears as . . . well, essentially as puppets. Holding the auricular appendages upright, she makes them dance, exchange witty dialogue, or even engage in wild battles *à la* Punch and Judy.

Not that I am vain about the black beauties—another common sobriquet for ears that shimmer and flow like rivers of living velvet. No, no, no.

Trying to be a good sport, I offered up my ears by lifting them to the sides. Lucky I did, for our svelte thespian's mood was tender, not teasing. Musetta has a special, soothing gesture for each of us. For the Twins, she combs and dresses their hair. For Gubbins, a buff and polish, and for Rumple, the occasional hug. For me: tender attention to my noggin and its auditory adjuncts.

She began to gently massage my ears and scalp. Between us, Ladies and Gentlemen, the treatment is heavenly. I recommend it highly, even to those with ears of, ahem, the minimalist, human variety.

I leaned back and closed my eyes, indulging.

"You know, my bunny-headed buddy," mused massaging Musetta, "Something about this 'Agnes' really unnerved us."

"Agnes?" I grunted. Between Musetta's massaging fingers and the warmth of the fire on my toes, I was already nodding off. Nodding off to *Sleepy Town*, to use the Twins' argot.

"Agnes—the new nanny. She was glum, but it was more than that. She . . . She seemed to be thinking unfriendly thoughts."

That dragged me back to reality for a moment.

"Unfriendly thoughts—in this house?!"

"I know! And the way she looked at little Bingo—" Musetta's hands froze, mid-massage.

"Yes?"

"She looked at him with sullen, covetous eyes."

Sullen, covetous eyes. Spooky, yes, but what effect could a bad attitude have on our happy home? I leaned back in the chair and returned Musetta's hands to their current duty.

After all, I thought, Mother and Father sat together with Bingo in the snug drawing room downstairs. We Cozies enjoyed a fairly typical evening in our parlor in the window seat. Musetta's magic fingers drifted through the fur at my temples like a harpist playing a lullaby.

All seemed right with the . . . zzzzzzzzzz.

★   ★   ★

6

A Fairly Typical Cozy Segue

"Hey! No fair!"
"Thursby got candy in Sleepy Town!"

Before I was even fully awake, a pulling sensation alongside my twitching nose hinted at the evidence against me. I blinked my eyes and smacked my lips, coming out of my reverie.

I was still in my armchair at the hearth. The Twins stood before me, tugging on the sleeves of my dapper green jacket. Musetta occupied the armchair to my right, and Rumple had moved as near as he could between Musetta's chair and mine.

With Pudding curled up at his feet, Gubbins rested in the armchair on my left. His jumble of cogs, casings, sprockets, and springs glowed like a kaleidoscope of metallic hues. Copper, bronze, platinum, gold—all danced with reflected firelight.

Something, though, obscured my view on the same side as that pulling sensation. I reached up to discover the remnant crescent of an oversized, rainbow-swirl lollipop stuck to one side of my face.

"Don't worry girls," said Musetta, "I'm sure Thursby brought candy for everyone." Leaning forward, elbows on her knees, she raised her eyebrows and pursed her lips. "You did, didn't you? Bring some for everyone?"

Looking around, I smoothed my ears and straightened my jacket.

"Er . . . 'fraid not," I admitted.

"Ohhhhh, Thursby—and after I sent you off to sleep with a nice ear massage." Musetta clicked her tongue at me.

"I wasn't ready to come back yet when you woke me! I was about to—"

"Ohhhhh, Thursby," mimicked Gracie.

Ruby clicked her tongue.

"Ohhh, yourselves," I said, peeling the sticky crescent off of my face.

The others laughed, except for Gubbins. I think he was also enjoying a fireside nap. It's hard to tell sometimes. He doesn't close his eyes when he sleeps, you see—their whimsical design doesn't allow for it. But a soft hum of contentment purred somewhere in his middle.

I laughed along with the others. There are seldom bad feelings between nursery figments. After all, if any Cozy wanted a lolly, or hot cocoa, or ice cream, or any other sweet prevalent in children's dreams, it's only a nap away.

And how, you may ask, does that little trick work?

To paraphrase the rule—and omitting a certain footnote about fireworks, all stemming from one exaggerated incident in which I was really only a bystander . . . *ahem* . . . The rule states that, while serving in the real world, a Cozy may make personal use of items left behind in the world of dreams.

You see, although Cozies do not need to sleep like people do, when we do sleep, we dream. Those dreams transport us back to the world of children's dreams. There we enjoy something like a vacation from the workaday world of the nursery. We can also collect supplies—*le materiél des rêves* that decorates our parlor, outfits us for activities, and provides us with sweets. It is all the produce of children's dreams.

Thankfully, sleeping children aren't any better about putting away their toys than children who are awake.

Some things, like oversized, rainbow-swirl lollies—a dream-world staple—are easy to come by. Other items are more rare, like, just for example, tugboat winches.

The supplies, of course, come pre-sized for Cozies. As you can see, the world of dreams runs at a scale of about one to twelve. After all, Cozies aren't miniature in the dream world, ha, ha. That would be silly.

After we'd all had our laugh and the lolly was released from my face fur, the Twins got back to their reason for awakening me in the first place.

"Why didn't you come downstairs with us today?" asked the twin on the right, followed by the twin on the left:

"Why do you spend so much time with Bingo's great-grandpa?"

"Great-grandfather was the child who made me up," I explained to the girls as they took seats on the hearthside rug. Their pink tutus deepened almost to red with the firelight behind them.

The Twins pulled Pudding over between them. The mouse growled softly, then rolled onto her back for a belly rub.

I continued, "Just as Great-grandfather's sister, when she was a little girl, was the one who made up Musetta."

"Great-grandmother!" exclaimed Gracie.

Musetta took that one. "No, dear. Great-grandfather's little sister, Myrtle, was Bingo's great-grand-aunt."

The Twins looked at one another, each scrunching up one side of her face in confusion.

"Of course," I went on, "the two of you sprang from Mother's imagination, when she was a tiny thing. And of all the grown-up people, don't you feel a special love for Mother?"

"Yes!" cheered the Twins with a loving flutter of their wings.

"That's how I feel about Great-grandfather. I watched over him as a little tyke in our very same nursery. I watched him grow up, and I've watched him grow old. He's very special to me."

Musetta's lips spread into a slightly mischievous smile. "So special," she divulged, "that Thursby once dared to go on a voyage at sea to stay with Great-grandfather."

"A voyage at sea?!" blurted Gracie.

"You never told us you went to sea!" cried Ruby.

"Wait," Gracie questioned, "the real sea?"

"Or do you mean the pond in the garden?"

"Oh, the real sea," said Musetta. "Where pirates sail!"

"Pirates!"

"Yes, well, that was the idea," I said. "Perhaps I'd better explain."

You see where this is going, don't you, Ladies and Gentlemen? Yes, a story within a story. A slight detour, but it was that evening after Agnes the nanny entered our lives that I first related the story of my voyage to the Twins.

Most importantly, that fireside chat planted a seed in our little Cozy minds—the seed of an inkling of an idea of a possibility—of doing something about something. Of actually making a difference in the world around us. You will hear soon how fortunate it was that that seed had begun to germinate.

First, though, with your permission, I will relate my seafaring saga—a tale I call, *The Sea Will Swallow Us All.*

(Flip-chart Exhibit #3: "Aivasovsky's Storm at Sea")

EXHIBIT #3

* * *

7

The Sea Will Swallow Us All

For now I will refer to Great-grandfather by his childhood nickname—Augie, short for Augustus.

Augie was little more than a boy when one night he came home very late. He wore a sailor's uniform of blue wool with white piping. He had tied his school clothes into a bundle.

Instead of going to school, Augie had ridden off and joined the Navy. He announced to the family that he was going to sea to fight pirates.

I told you he was a rascal.

Augie's mother—Bingo's great-great-grandmother—cried her heart out. After all, Augie was not really old enough to volunteer, not officially. He had grown quite tall, but he was still very young. Why, he couldn't even grow his muttonchops yet! Not that human whiskers are much of a substitute for the real thing . . .

(pause for a smoothing of whiskers)

. . . but they are at least a symbol of manhood.

Great-great-grandmother's protests were to no avail. Augie's father would not allow his son to go back on his word.

After only a few days, Augie had to leave. A ship was going to take him somewhere far away.

I couldn't bear the thought of him going off to be in danger without me to watch over him. Why, only an instant had passed— or so it seemed—since he'd been a tiny lad with ringlets, riding his rocking horse in the nursery alcove.

On the morning of Augie's departure, his baggage was stacked in his room: a large steamer trunk, a footlocker, and a duffle bag. The trunk was still open. I climbed in and slipped down into the clothing and possessions. I found a comfortable place and settled in.

Soon enough, someone shut the trunk lid. We were off!

The first part of the journey, the sea remained calm. Days passed with hardly any sensation of movement. Of course, I remained tucked away in the trunk, buffered from the jostling one might expect when traveling great distances.

Since the trunk was undoubtedly stowed away in the deepest recesses of the ship, it was unlikely that I would get out until the voyage ended. So I could only imagine the smooth, endless sea, the exotic ports of call, and the dewy ocean breeze.

The calm seas did not last. A storm came suddenly and without warning. As the ship began to rock, my steamer trunk shifted, then started to slide. My trunk banged into other trunks in the baggage compartment.

The blows fell harder and harder. Wind and rain with the power of a hurricane battered the ship! At the mercy of the merciless storm, the steamer trunk crashed against the baggage-compartment walls—whump! Whump, whump, whump!

I pictured young Augie on deck in a rain slicker, pulling on ropes and battening down hatches and doing the other things that sailors do as waves wash over them.

The worst was yet to come. The trunk started to flip end over end! Spinning through the darkness inside the trunk, I knew that there could be but one explanation: A massive wave had struck the ship and rolled it over, dragging the vessel and hundreds of poor young sailors down into the murky depths. The sea will swallow us all, I thought. The sea will swallow us all!

My poor Augie!

Then, calm again. Silence. We were obviously below the surface now, in the silent depths below the storm.

Finally, under the weight of the ocean above, the steamer trunk burst open! I smoothed my ears, straightened my jacket, and prepared myself.

It occurred to me then that instead of cold, salty, seawater, the nooks and crannies around me had filled with light.

A girl's voice exclaimed, "There you are!" Something soft beside me started to move. I grabbed hold, and found myself lifted out of the steamer trunk.

"I thought I might find you here," said Augie's sister, Myrtle. She spoke not to me but to an old rag doll. I went unnoticed, clinging to the doll's yarn hair. Myrtle was already too old to see figments, of the nursery variety or otherwise, unless she was half asleep or better.

Still young enough, though, to keep dolls piled on her bed, she had come looking for a missing one in her brother's trunk.

"I can't believe Augie packed my doll in his storage trunk!" Myrtle complained. As I climbed up to her shoulder, she spotted a note pinned to the doll's blouse. She read it aloud: "Dear Sis — I told you to stay out of my things. — Your loving brother, Augie."

Myrtle slammed the trunk lid shut and ran up the cellar stairs to tell on that rascal of a brother of hers. I left her grousing in the kitchen and made my way up the back stairs to the nursery.

In those days, mind you, we had no Dinmont or other conveyance for speedy travel around the house. There was a cat, if I recall—Puffy, or Sluffy, or something-uffy. Cats, however, do not distinguish between the real and imaginary the way other creatures do. Not one feline in a thousand would let a five-inch-tall, rabbity fellow ride on its back, no matter how nattily dressed the fellow might be.

Our entry into the parlor was the same back then: Offset baseboards beneath the window-seat left a narrow wedge of an opening. I slipped inside.

Musetta stood on the oval rug practicing for her presentation, *History of the World in Mime*. Gubbins sat at his drafting table. He saw me first and emitted the trilling-bells sound that is his nom de Gubbins for Thursby.

(Here the speaker makes a high-pitched trilling sound, which the transcriptionist will represent henceforth as "Tr-r-r-r-r-r-r-!")

"Tr-r-r-r-r-r-r-!"

(The transcriptionist, taking notes nearby, pauses for a brief wiping of spectacles, as some damp- ness has accompanied the trilling.)

Musetta looked over her shoulder. "Greetings, mighty warrior," she deadpanned. "After three days, I figured you were doing battle with a pirate's parrot somewhere."

And that, Ladies and Gentlemen, is the embarrassing but true story of my so-called voyage at sea. I'd never even left our comfort- able country home. Rather than weeks, only a few days had passed, most of which time my steamer trunk had lain unmoved in Augie's bedroom. The hurricane had hit as the trunk was dragged down- stairs. The massive wave had struck when a servant accidentally let the trunk tumble down the cellar steps.

In summary, if I might be so bold as to quote from my most recent volume of poetry, *Thursbiana*, published in France and Quebec as *Pensées du Lapin Noir*:

What tricks imagination plays!

What frightful thoughts released!

Enough to make us fear a breeze

is some outrageous beast.

PART TWO

Enter the Villains

8

Agnes of the Horizontal Head

Returning to our main narrative.

Agnes, the new nanny, moved in the very next day. It was as if a shadow fell over the household.

"Woe!" bemoaned Musetta, collapsing onto our parlor settee. "Woe art we who hath received unto our bosom this burden, but of bosom unburdening, may not partake!"

She gave us a sidelong glance.

"Ah!" I responded. I applauded to encourage the others. "Bravissima, Musetta! Brava!"

"That was wonderful!" raved Ruby.

"It gave me chills!" agreed Gracie.

"Coo-coo! Coo-coo!" chimed Gubbins. In addition to substituting for laughter, his cuckoo-clock chimes apply to general approval and enjoyment. At least I hope they do. Otherwise, Gubbins has been laughing in our faces for years. Ha, ha.

Hm.

Musetta sat up into a less distraught pose, giving short bows of the head. "Thank you. Thank you all. But there isn't anything we can do, and it's driving me crazy."

The Twins climbed onto the settee with Musetta, one on each side. Gracie asked, "What do you mean 'do,' Musetta?"

Ruby joined, "You mean like, perform on the window sill?"

"Or watch clouds?"

"Or snuggle Bingo to help him sleep?"

"*Like* snuggling Bingo," said Musetta. "But something more. Something like . . ." Musetta looked at me as if I might finish her thought.

I was stumped. Together we looked at Gubbins.

A whirring sound started to build inside him, but fell away. A miniature winch-wheel on his upper back pulled two wires attached to his shoulders inward, then let them drop. In other words, Gubbins shrugged.

"Like when Thursby got into the trunk?" suggested Gracie.

"Yes!" said Musetta and I together.

"You were going to fight pirate parrots!" Ruby proclaimed proudly. What a sweetheart.

"Something like that," I said. "To be honest, I had no clue what I'd do if I ended up at sea. After all, one wouldn't sing lullabies for a pirate-fighting sailor."

Gracie was incredulous. "Pirate fighters don't get lullabies?!"

"Poor little pirate fighters," said Ruby with a frown.

We all sat quietly for a moment, baffled by this concept of doing something about something. As you might have guessed, Cozies are not exactly action-oriented. What with being imaginary and living in a nursery and all.

Suddenly Rumple started to applaud. He was looking at Musetta.

"I do believe he's praising your performance," I guessed. "'Woe art we . . .'?"

"Oh!" Musetta stood and gave our soft, baby-blue friend a hug. "Thanks, Rumply-wumply!"

"Maybe there isn't anything that needs to be done about Agnes," I suggested. "After all, we have no proof that she's scary. We only have a bad feeling."

"The proof is in her eyes," Musetta pressed. "Her sullen, covetous eyes."

"Ah yes. The eyes."

"They're sullen," said Gracie.

"And covetous," added Ruby.

Having seen Agnes for the first time earlier in the day, I had to admit that our dramaturge's description was accurate.

Strangely enough, the shape of the nanny's head added to her unnerving aura. Most humans' heads, of course, are generally oval in shape. That oval usually extends up from the neck in a vertical position, like a potato standing on one end. Agnes's head, on the other hand, was oval-shaped in a horizontal position—that is to say, longer from ear to ear than from chin to crown.

Not that there is anything wrong with horizontal-headed people! Why, some of my best imaginary friends have horizontal heads. With Agnes, though, the shape only accentuated the constant frown on her mouth. Her whole head frowned.

Then there was her covetousness, revealed mainly in the way her gaze lingered on things—the household finery, Mother's jewelry, Father's handsome face. Most disturbing was the way Agnes would fix her jealous stare on little Bingo. Even the grabby way she would take Bingo into her arms seemed covetous, like she was snatching him away.

Not wanting to inspire panic, I said nothing more on the subject. In my mind, however, there was little doubt: The arrival of Agnes of the Horizontal Head spelled trouble.

⋆   ⋆   ⋆

9

A Brief Discourse on Figmentology

You might be wondering why we Cozies found the mere presence of a suspicious person so worrisome. Understandably, humans take for granted the ability to control their physical surroundings. So let us examine further the science of figmentology.

If my assistant would be so kind . . .

(Flip-chart Exhibit #4: "Comparison Diagram")

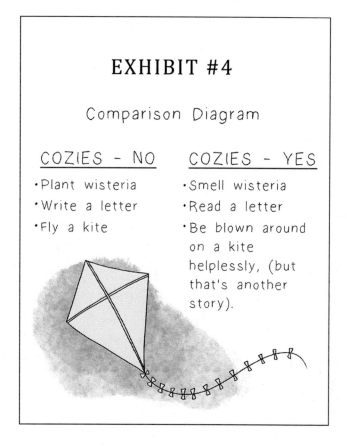

EXHIBIT #4

Comparison Diagram

COZIES - NO

•Plant wisteria
•Write a letter
•Fly a kite

COZIES - YES

•Smell wisteria
•Read a letter
•Be blown around on a kite helplessly, (but that's another story).

As we've discussed, in most cases nursery figments cannot affect the so-called real world. Absent moonlight or its various derivatives, we Cozies could not type a letter on the fine black typewriter in Father's study. The letter *T*, for example—long considered the most aristocratic of letters—would remain untyped.

Just the same, if we Cozies were in Father's study on a summer afternoon and a breeze swirled in from the garden window, we would enjoy its refreshing caress. The scent of wisteria would make our nostrils flare and whiskers twitch as much as anyone's. What's more, if that ambrosial breeze billowed just right, the Twins might enjoy a ride on sheets of paper scooting across Father's mahogany desk.

All this is discussed in my pamphlet, *Scents and Sans Ability: A Theoretical Analysis of the Relationship Between Imaginary Beings and the Natural World, A Lop-eared Perspective*. Please see the convention organizers for ordering information.

For our purposes, a summary will do: The natural world and the world of dreams share some qualities, but not all, by any means.

When you think about it, humans can also move from one world to another without truly joining it. A person might swim underwater, but said person can't breathe there, or talk to the fish. Which is too bad, as I am reliably informed that fish have formidable senses of humor. Particularly carp.

But enough of the science lesson, hm?

★   ★   ★

10

The Next First Tuesday of the Month

Early spring moved toward mid-spring one day at a time, then one week at a time, and finally, not unexpectedly, by a full month.

With the new nanny available, Bingo spent less time with Mother. Father had told Mother that she needed her rest. He wanted her to let Agnes care for Bingo. Mother did not seem ill, so we weren't sure why she would need more rest than before. Mother even seemed to have put on weight, mainly through the middle. She had a healthy glow about her.

As habitual human watchers, Mother's condition seemed familiar to us. We sensed, however, that this touched on those aspects of "reality" that Cozies prefer to ignore. So we simply went about our business.

Our business at night, of course, was to watch over and comfort Bingo. Poor tyke. The less time he spent with Mother, the less happy he was. Was it not for our round-the-clock work, if I do say so myself, he wouldn't have had a single good night's sleep. We sang lullabies, we danced, we whispered happy, dreamy tales into his little pink ears.

During the daytime, we went on with our usual activities. Several days were warm and clear enough for Dinmont rides in the garden. We made our first trip of the new year to the rooftop for cloud gazing. And the Spring Gallery Stroll was a distinct success, with works presented by each of the Cozies. Rumple's entry was actually the product of a sneeze. But who were we to question an artist's choice of medium?

The next first Tuesday of the month finally arrived—time, at last, for the long delayed premiere of *Pining Maiden, Part III.* It was not raining this time. In fact, beyond the nursery windows the weather was quite clear.

This calm weather surprised us. The newspaper—which I would read at the breakfast table from Father's shoulder—had reported that storms were expected throughout the region all week.

Mother, Father, Bingo, and Dandie were away visiting neighbors for the day. Michael had taken the family on their outing in the big carriage. Michael was a lanky, quiet human who wore many hats around the estate, including stable keeper, chauffeur, and husband of Bridie the housekeeper.

The day-trippers had dropped Bridie in town to do the shopping. Abigail the cook had the day off. This meant that, other than Great-grandfather, who was napping, the only human in the house was Agnes. We had, I must admit, grown less wary of Agnes over the weeks. Other than her sullen and covetous eyes, she hadn't done anything scary . . . yet.

Pudding benefitted from the unusual lack of humans and terriers. She sat between Gubbins and I on the window seat, wagging her tail and panting. These were new additions to her caninean repertoire.

"Sproing!" sang the Twins, adding sound effects to their latest game. They'd discovered that they could bounce from the big burgundy pillow, off of Rumple, and to the window-seat cushion. Rumple's little black eyes widened with surprise every time.

"Girls," I said. "Are you certain you're not tormenting poor Rumple?"

"He likes it!" declared Gracie as Ruby took a bounce off of Rumple's head.

"Yes, he—" started Ruby in midair, then she came down right on her rump on the cushion. "Oof!" Immediately she looked over her shoulder and past her fluttering left wing to share a good giggle with Gracie.

Musetta had added a dramatic flair to the opening: She stood on the sill facing the window, her back to us, her head bowed. She turned suddenly with dramatic flair, raising her arms slightly, then dropping them slowly to her sides.

The Twins scurried excitedly to their places on the pillow.

A hush fell over the audience.

*   *   *

11

Seven Flying Fays
and One Brutish Lout

Swoosh! A bright white light flew past Musetta's head, close enough to fan the golden plume of her headdress. Musetta tried her best to ignore it. She turned her head to one side to begin, but then: Swoosh! Swoosh-swoosh! Swoosh-swoosh-swoosh!

Gracie jumped up and pointed. "The Flying Fays are inside!"

"Is that allowed?" asked Ruby.

(murmuring in the audience)

"Allowed?" said Musetta with arms akimbo. "Sure, why not? Never happened before, not in all these years, but now, at this moment, they decide to—"

(The murmuring in the audience increases.)

Hm? The Flying Fays? Why, I'm sure I described them earlier, what?

(The speaker leafs through his notes.)

Ah! My apologies, Ladies and Gentlemen. The Flying Fays, as we call those ethereal beings, play a key role in our story. Let's take a moment to discuss them.

Before certain events, which we will discuss momentarily, all I could say about the Flying Fays was that there were seven of them. To me they appeared to be nothing more than small, bright lights that could fly. As far as I knew they had no more to do with Cozies, or our mission, than the fireflies who, in summer months, also decorated the garden.

Mainly the Flying Fays resided in the air space outside the nursery windows. On many a warm summer eve, they would entertain us with their antics. Flying in a straight line or a geese-like V-formation, they'd begin the evening at a cool-green glow. To complement the sunset, they would morph through shades of pink and purple. As night fell they would end back at their basic star-white light. With their loop-the-loops, spirals, and zigzags, they gave us our own private fireworks show.

The Fays appear to be intrigued by the activities of others. Their fascination extends equally to creatures from the real world, such as humans, beings from the dream world, such as Cozies, and creatures of both the real and imaginary worlds, such as hummingbirds.

Later we learned that these pixies or sprites or fairies or whatever generic term one prefers, had lived in the real world longer than any of us except Gubbins. This was not by chance, as you shall hear.

After buzzing Musetta on that second first Tuesday of the month, our airborne *amici* zipped up and down in a jagged line right in front of us. They were displaying displeasure as distinctly as a fist pounding a table top.

"Look!" Gracie pointed out as the Fays shot toward the doorway and then back again. "They're changing color!"

"They're turning red!" observed Ruby.

"Something must've really irked our little night lights," said Musetta.

The words were no more out of her mouth than she and I shot glances at each other and simultaneously repeated, "Irked!" Musetta hopped down from the sill and came over beside Gubbins and me.

As if they'd read our minds, or we had read theirs, or perhaps some simultaneous mind-reading had occurred, the Fays flew into a horizontal-oval formation. The floating oval then deflated in the middle and dropped on the sides to a frown shape.

"Tik-whirrrrrrrr," sounded Gubbins, with the *whirrrrrrr* falling away to a slow, low growl—his moniker for Agnes the nanny.

"Agnes!" gasped Musetta and I and the Twins all together.

With that the Fays formed an arrow shape and flew again toward the doorway. There, floating in midair, the brightness of their little red lights began to pulsate.

"They want us to follow them!" shouted the Twins.

Rumple certainly wasn't hesitating. Mesmerized by the Fays' flashing arrow, he stepped over the edge of the window seat without pausing to look down. Not unexpectedly, he dropped straight to the floor.

Fortunately, the window seat was low enough that we each had our own method for quick descents. As noted, Rumple would fall and bounce. Not exactly a *method* really, but it got him there. After several bounces and a roll he was up and toddling after the Fays.

I used my umbrella, as previously described.

Musetta's skirt provided an umbrella-like service. It would billow out in the shape of a turned-over flower vase. With Musetta's help, the Twins' wings—although not fit for actual take-off—provided enough drag for a short drop.

Musetta held hands with the girls, one on each side. "One, two, three—jump!"

"Weeeeeeeeeee!"

When they touched down, Musetta absorbed the initial impact with her long legs and helped the Twins to land more gently.

Gubbins' mechanical legs can extend out to absorb the shock of the leap when necessary, though it results in a painfully metallic squeaking. This time, though, he returned Pudding to the parlor through a small mouse hole behind the window-seat cushion. He then joined us through the offset baseboards.

"Those Flying Fays are full of surprises," Musetta said sardonically as we ran out of the alcove and across the corner of the nursery rug. She was a might miffed at the second interruption of her opus.

"To be honest," I admitted, "for a decade or two, I thought they were bugs!"

The long hallway opened up to the stairhall below. We lined up along the base of the stairway rail.

"A man!" yelled Gracie.

"Who's *that*?!" cried Ruby.

Alas, there was no answer to give, for the man was a stranger. A stranger in our house, with Mother and Father and Bridie and Michael and Abigail the cook all away. Shock and chagrin, ladies and gentlemen! That's what we felt—shock and chagrin.

Not only was the man a stranger, but a stranger whom one could only describe as a brutish lout. Unkempt, slouching, with that dull stare usually seen only in bovine species, although bovines don't usually complement their stares with a sneer. Except for a Jersey cow named Hazel who grazed on the next-door pasture. Hazel sneered constantly with an arrogance that is particularly unbecoming in a milk cow.

The stranger's sneer, though, was hateful, not arrogant. His upper lips . . . Forgive me, I mean his upper *lip*—I forget that not everyone is blessed with two upper lips. His upper lip retracted like a bristly curtain, exposing a wall of unhealthy, sticky-looking gums. Below this unattractive display, his lower lip twisted into a frown.

The brutish lout shared Agnes's horizontal-headedness. This surprised us, given that Agnes had been the first human we'd seen sporting that trait.

Agnes and the brutish lout whispered to each other, despite the fact that, as far as they knew, no one other than napping Great-grandfather was home.

Although eavesdropping is seldom acceptable, there are exceptions. Our duty to Bingo made this such an exception. We listened intently.

★   ★   ★

12

A Disturbing Encounter

"**M**umble mumble mumble," said Agnes to the brutish lout. Not literally of course. It only sounded like that due to the duo's low volume.

Their horizontal heads practically touched as Agnes and the brutish lout muttered mysteriously. Their shifty eyes darted back and forth, their gazes glancing around the stairhall. Perhaps they worried that someone might leap from behind the grandfather clock or hall tree and shout *Ah-hah! We've caught you, you brutish lout and suspicious-seeming nanny!*

"Mumble!" hissed the lout with an extra-sneer-filled sneer at Agnes.

Agnes lowered her head with extra-sullen sullenness.

The brutish lout continued, "Awright. Mumble, mumble, place in the Big City, mumble."

With that, as they say in floppy-eared circles, our ears stood up like a straight-eared rabbit's. I drew a sudden breath. Musetta whispered "Oh!" Gubbins whirred with worry, and the Twins repeated the fearful words, their little voices on the verge of panic: "The Big City!"

The Flying Fays, watching from above, flew into a tizzy. Their little line of red lights spiraled up near the ceiling, then down again, finishing with another fist-pounding zigzag.

Only Rumple was spared the general angst. By virtue of his innocence about such things, the phrase held little meaning for him. Also, he was facing the wrong direction altogether.

Why, you may ask, all the fuss about the Big City?

Of we Cozies, only Gubbins had been to the Big City. He had lived there long ago, before the family moved to the country. He never spoke about it, and when pressed, he would fall into a Gubbinsly panic. That means that his head tilts on its spring-like base, twists to one side with a painful grating-metal sound, then snaps back the other way in short jerks, while his lower-jaw piece opens and shuts with a worrisome wah-wah-wah sound. It is highly disturbing, so we avoid the subject for both Gubbins' sake and ours.

Human references to the Big City only added to our impression of the place. They would speak of people locking their doors at night. They would refer to people *escaping* the city for the country. And when Father returned from business trips, he would describe the Big City with words like *crazy* and *crowded*, *noisy* and *nuts*, *dirty* and . . . *dangerous*.

"Mumble?" asked Agnes, turning quickly to look at the brutish lout full on.

"Mumble," confirmed the lout with a slow nod. "Mumble take the kid mumble-mumble."

Take the kid: The words threw us all into a full-fledged panic. Unfortunately, panic is no more attractive in cute little imaginary beings than in humans. Well, not much more attractive.

"Aaaaaaaaaaaaaaa!" screamed the Twins. Pulling the sides of their hair, they ran in circles until they bounced—whump!—smack into each other. Then they jumped up, hugged each other cheek to cheek, and alternated short panicky screams. "Aaaaaa!" "Aaaaaa!" "Aaaaaa!" And so forth.

Gubbins fell into a true Gubbinsly panic, complete with grating-metal sounds and "wah-wah-wah" jaw noises.

The Fays shot this way and that like a trapped bird looking for an exit.

Whether or not he understood it, the general panic even affected poor Rumple. He ran straight across the hallway until he bumped into the wall. There he remained, staring ahead. Evidently the simplicity of this view comforted him.

While all this was going on, Musetta and I bickered—that unfortunate habit of brothers, sisters, spouses, and close friends in moments of stress: "Well, Mister Rabbit Head, I told you there was something about her!" "You weren't exactly full of ideas yourself, Miss Woe-art-we!" "I'm a thespian beauty, not a tactician!" "And I'm a lagomorph poet, not a gendarme!" "Oh, of course—a scholar when you want to be a know-it-all, a poet when you want to be lazy!" "If that's not the pot calling the kettle slack!"

The front door slammed. The noise shocked us out of our separate panics and into silence. The brutish lout had left.

Musetta and I paused, looking sheepishly at one another. She spoke first.

"I'm scared," she said.

I smoothed my ears, then nodded. "Me, too."

★ ★ ★

13

A Smiling Friend

The Moon comforted us that night. Nearly full, our friend floated crisp and bright in the sky outside the nursery window. The calm smile and kind eyes let us know, in that quiet way, that everything would be all right.

Correct me if I am wrong, but I gather that humans cannot actually see the Moon's face, except as gray blotches on a bright white background. Of course, people can *imagine* the Moon's face. We know this because drawings and paintings throughout the ages have depicted the great orb's benign expression.

To Cozies, the notion that the Moon is giant floating rock, or even an immense ball of cheese, is like calling the *Mona Lisa* a few handfuls of paint on a slab of wood. What the Moon is made of, is not the point. The Moon is tides and tenderness, light and life, majesty and magic.

The Moon's fullness and closeness that night was a happy coincidence. We needed any comfort we could get after the disturbing encounter. All afternoon and evening we'd tried to convince ourselves that the overheard snippets of conversation had meant nothing. Still, we were all glad when Bingo, and Mother and Father, and the others all arrived safely home.

When Mother and Father were home, it didn't seem possible that anything could go wrong.

Just the same, we all snuggled in around Bingo in the crib that night. Rumple was happy as a clam with one of Bingo's arms around him. The Twins nestled in beside the boy's head. Musetta and I sat on the baby blanket like two people enjoying a moonlit picnic.

Gubbins sat on the rail at the foot of the crib, keeping watch.

"Yes," Musetta piped up—as if we'd just been talking about it, although we had not been for an hour or so—"we overreacted. I'm sure of it."

I tried to agree. "I'm certain as well. We heard blurbs out of context. Why, they were probably talking about a different child altogether."

"Certainly makes one think, though. What would we do if something threatened Bingo?"

"The children in the household have faced dangers before. Remember when Mother's sister had scarlet fever? We simply have to do our duty, comfort the children as best we can, and accept that there is nothing more that we can do."

"Mm." Musetta sounded unconvinced. "What could a little band of nursery figments do to thwart a crime?"

"Exactly."

We went back to moonbathing.

Despite our attempts at reassuring each other, even the Moon seemed less at ease than usual. The deep, dark eyes seemed to be peering through the clear night sky and off into the distance. Perhaps, I thought, a storm waits on the horizon.

How true that would turn out to be.

*   *   *

14

Treachery and Malefaction

In the very early morning hours, before sunrise, there was a stir-ring in the house.

It began as a soft squeaking. At first I thought it was Pudding, who'd perhaps found an intriguing crumb. I lifted my head drows-ily from the baby blanket. Bingo slept peacefully.

I smoothed out my ear against the blanket and lowered my head.

"Tr-r-r-r-r-r-r-." The soft trilling came from Gubbins, trying to get my attention. I leapt up. Gubbins was still seated on the rail at the foot of the crib. Musetta was seated beside him. They were cocking their heads, listening.

The Twins were playing a patty-cake game on the other side of Bingo. Rumple was asleep, and appeared to be enjoying a good dream-holiday. Rumple slept more than the rest of us. No doubt it provided a respite from this befuddling reality.

I heard the squeaking again and knew it was not Pudding. Slow creaking sounds made their way down the drop-down staircase from the attic bedroom—*footsteps*. Footsteps that fell furtively, stealthily.

"Agnes!" I whispered.

"What could she be up to?" said Musetta.

Silence again. Or was that a nightgown hem shuffling on the hallway runner?

The nursery doorknob turned slowly. It caught the Twins' attention.

"What's that?" asked Gracie, climbing over Bingo.

"Is it morning?" asked Ruby, looking at the still-dark window.

A wide, pale face peeked into the room. Shadows in the already dark room painted deep rings around the eyes and deepened the scowl of the mouth.

"Aaaaaaaaaaaa!" screamed the Twins.

Then Gracie noticed, "Oh, it's only Agnes."

"Agnes?!" cried Ruby, recalling the disturbing encounter.

"Aaaaaaaaaaaa!"

Agnes carried no lamp. She crept in and tiptoed past the crib to the window-seat alcove. Kneeling on the seat, she opened the window wide and peered outside.

I leapt through the crib rail posts and opened my umbrella to slow my drop. Once on the floor, I ran over and started climbing the decorative edging up to the window seat.

"Psst!" Agnes whispered loudly. "You down there?"

"Yeah I'm down here! What took you?" came another voice. No mistaking it: the voice of the brutish lout.

Whump! The top rails of the family's ladder, which usually rested behind the garden shed, thudded against the exterior sill of the nursery window.

Ruby and Gracie hugged each other tightly.

It struck me—belatedly, I admit, but treachery and malefaction are not familiar to a nursery figment—that Agnes was not acting like a criminal, she *was* a criminal!

"Wake the baby!" I cried as I stepped from the decorative edging to the window sill.

Without hesitation, Gubbins jumped from crib rail to blankie. By the time he landed, his alarm bell rang loudly. After knowing

Gubbins for the better part of a century at that point, that was the first time I'd heard his alarm. There was no missing it: Any Cozy or small child within a mile would hear it.

Gubbins ran right up onto Bingo's chest. The boy stirred. Gubbins waved his arms wildly. In his excitement, Gubbins' whole figure seemed to move—tiny wheels spun and hummed, flaps opened and closed, sprockets clicked and ticked.

I should mention here that little Bingo, despite his tender age, possessed an extremely good-natured personality. Unfortunately, some commendable traits are not handy in emergencies. Instead of screeching and wailing, Bingo simply giggled when he spotted the arm-waving, alarm-sounding, mechanized figment standing on him.

"Goobee!" chirped the boy.

Musetta and the Twins joined in the child-riling effort. Scaring a small child, though, is a foreign concept for Cozies. We simply weren't any good at it.

The brutish lout's brutishly loutish face popped up outside the window. To our surprise, the Flying Fays appeared right along with him. They were busily buzzing the lout's horizontal cranium like miniature fighter planes on the attack.

No, there were no such things as fighter planes in those days. But I stand by my simile.

Once they saw what was happening inside, the light-sprites joined the effort to make Bingo cry out. The flying lights, though, probably only added to what Bingo must have seen as a spontaneously festive occasion.

"Hand me the brat," the brutish lout whispered.

Agnes hesitated. She lowered her eyes, then glanced sullenly toward the crib.

"Look—" she started to say—

"You look!" hissed the lout. He reached right into the room and grabbed Agnes roughly by one arm. "Hand me that brat.*Now.*"

Agnes lowered her eyes again and nodded. The lout released her. Agnes went to the crib and lifted Bingo out, along with the baby blankie. This pulled the carpet, so to speak, out from under my fellow Cozies. They spilled back into the crib.

Excited to join the wild dance of his imaginary friends, Bingo seemed pleased to see even Agnes. He raised his little arms and waved them about while chattering away. "Goobee rumshaw ah bizoo," he explained happily to the kidnapping conspirator. "Bumple schnap, murfle Moosie waddle frumbee."

Even when Agnes handed him off to the brutish lout—still enjoying what probably seemed like a strange dream—the trusting babe said only, "Oop a daisy!"

At that moment, I leaped off of the window sill and grabbed ahold of the blanket. I had no idea what to do if carried off with Bingo; I acted by instinct alone. In any event, the warm softness of the blanket must have offended the brutish lout's nature. He tore the blankie off of Bingo and tossed it, and me, back into the nursery.

Agnes shut the window quickly behind them.

All we heard from Bingo outside the window was one final word as the brutish lout carried him down the ladder. "Horsey?" said Bingo in a small voice—a voice filling with fear.

Hunched over, gaze downcast, Agnes stole from the room like a guilty shadow.

That, Ladies and Gentlemen, might have been the last we ever saw of our beloved Bingo. There is a fine line between tragedy and comedy; the decision of an instant can decide forever to which side of that line we drop. In this instance, Bingo's fate may well have hinged on the quick thinking of a single Cozy. I speak of a Cozy who, only a few hours before, had bemoaned again the helplessness of figmental beings in this world.

(The speaker pauses and steps away from his podium to signal the coming break.)

But that part of our story must wait. It is time for our midmorning comfort break. I invite you to stretch your legs and enjoy some of the refreshments provided by our sponsor, Jen and Barry's Bath Soap. "Jen and Barry's will leave your skin feeling as smooth as ice cream, but far less sticky."

We will begin again in twenty minutes. Hm. We're running a bit late. Let's try to keep it to fifteen, shall we? Thank you.

(applause, followed by break)

PART THREE

Doing Something
About Something

15

A Leader Is Born

Hello—in the back there? I say, those of you there in the back of the hall, from the *Absinthe* lecture. While I understand how the sight of a five-inch tall, rabbit-headed speaker might intrigue you, these seats are reserved exclusively for the *Imagination* conference. Please return to the Matterhorn Room.

(The speaker waits for a number of pallid and dazed persons dressed primarily in black to file out. The registered attendees take their seats.)

Hopefully that will be the last disruption. Perhaps I should speak with the folks next door about making a paid appearance at their next conference! Ha, ha.

(laughter from the audience)

Hm.

(The speaker takes a moment to jot down a note.)

Now then. From this point forward, you may notice that I will from time to time discuss things that do not stem from my own memory. These are matters, as they say in the study of Law, about which I have "no personal knowledge." Since the main subject of this lecture is imagination, let me assure you that any information beyond my own ken stems from research, and not through fictionalizing by a certain nattily dressed, lop-eared gent.

My fellow Cozies, obviously, told me about their experiences in subsequent conversations. Overheard human gossip and newspaper reports provided additional perspectives and satisfied much of our curiosity. The tale, I believe, enjoys greater depth when all points of view are taken into account.

Too many points of view at once, however, can be confusing. For that reason, before the break I took the liberty of omitting the experiences of the Flying Fays just before the kidnapping mêlée.

The Fays first came across the brutish lout in the garden. They started buzzing the trespasser while he crept through the grounds to the back garden. Their harassment, while well-intentioned, remained ineffectual. By that time of the early morning the Moon's arc had carried our primary source of moonlight far away. So the loutish one remained unaware of the swarming sprites.

I've already described Bingo's reaction to our panicked efforts to make him cry. To his toddler's eyes, it must have seemed a middle-of-the-night party, with ringing bells, hooting and hollering, and swirling lights.

What a shock it must have been when the little tyke found himself suddenly out in the cold, dark night, carried down a ladder by a nefarious stranger.

The slamming window dealt a blow to us as well. Absolute silence fell over us. Gubbins' alarm stopped. The shouts ended. The Fays dropped like dimming cinders to the floor.

We froze, dumbfounded, not believing the reality of what had happened. It is one thing to have a sense of foreboding. It is quite another thing to have an emergency of the worst sort hit you squarely in the face like an unexpected baseball.

"What happened to Bingo?" asked Gracie in the tiniest of tiny voices.

"Wha—" squeaked Ruby, unable to even echo her twin.

Rumple peeked under one corner of Bingo's pillow, as if the child might be hiding there.

From my spot on the floor of the nursery where I'd been flung along with Bingo's blankie, I looked up at Musetta. She stood along the top of the crib's headboard, staring at the black and silent windows. Her usual placid expression had been replaced with—

Wait, I thought. In her face I did not see grief or fear or any other expected emotion. Her dark red lips curled down deeply at the ends. The nostrils of her aquiline nose flared. Her kohled eyes squinted.

She is *angry*, I realized.

"THEY TOOK OUR BINGO!" roared Musetta with the fury of the Furies. She ran along the crib rail to the footboard and swung one gloved hand out to point at the door. "FLY, FAYS, FLY!" she commanded.

The Fays zipped into the air and started speeding haphazardly this way and that. They flew with such speed that their light trail wove a web of illumination in the nursery.

Pixies, not unexpectedly, are mercurial beings. As such, logical progression of thought is not their forté. The Fays understood Musetta's command, and they knew she meant right now. They did not, however, immediately understand the purpose.

"FOLLOW THEM!" Musetta clarified in none too patient a tone.

The Fays shot under the door to exit the room. The rest of us made our way back up to the inside window sill. I was closest and got there first, but already the Fays had flown downstairs and up and out the chimney. Their light trail curved broadly out over the next-door pasture and toward the road leading to . . . the Big City.

*   *   *

16

The Darkest Hours

The next few hours, we waited. We sat in the empty crib as if we could wish our little boy back home and safe again. The hours seemed like years.

Those hours must have passed just as slowly for Agnes, tormented by guilt in her room upstairs. Knowing that she would soon have to face Mother and Father. That she would have to tell those good people that their beloved baby had been snatched away into the night. That she would have to pretend to be as shocked as they would be.

Finally, at the first sign of morning light, we heard Agnes climbing back down from her attic room and toward the nursery. She opened the door . . . or at least, someone who looked like her did.

"Is that Agnes?" asked Gracie.

"She looks old," Ruby stated plainly.

It was true. In a few hours, the traitorous nanny appeared to have aged. Around a haggard face, frightful shocks of hair sprouted, as if teased out in a silent, guilty fit.

Agnes shuffled over to the crib and looked in, as if the brutish lout might've felt the same misgivings and brought the boy home. She sank to her knees beside the crib and struggled to stifle the sound of deep, sorrowful sobs.

After a bit, she drew herself up and opened the window. The ladder still stood ominously against the sill. Agnes took a deep breath and ran from the room.

(The speaker lowers his head. His ears hang forward, partly covering his face. After a moment, he smooths his ears back and dries his eyes.)

Forgive me, Ladies and Gentlemen, if I decline to relate in detail the painful events of the next few hours. Despite the passing of many years, to this day it is too hard to talk about. The shameful lies of Agnes, whose sheepish distress shored up her pretense. Mother's wailing, and the way she held her round tummy as she fainted into Father's arms. The mournful Gaelic oaths of Bridie. A house filled with panicked shouts and searching.

All this, we Cozies knew, was for naught. Kidnapper and kid were long gone.

Abigail the cook found Dandie in the pantry, very thirsty and badly needing to run outside. One time before, Dandie had been trapped in there by accident. I recalled having overheard Abigail tell Agnes about it. No doubt Agnes had shut the poor dog away to prevent him from barking at strange noises.

Soon the police arrived. Some wore uniforms of dark blue that reminded me of Augie's naval uniform of years long past. Others were dressed in nice suits. The arrival of these professionals was reassuring. That is, until Musetta returned from the family's drawing room to our parlor.

"They don't have a clue that Agnes was in on it!" she told us.

Over a quivering lower lip, Gracie cried, "We'll never see Bingo again!"

"Never," wept Ruby quietly.

"Don't start that again," said Musetta in a new, commanding tone.

Gracie lifted her little arms in a palms-up shrug and said, "What can we do?"

Without looking up, Ruby shook her head and echoed Gracie's shrug.

Rumple patted Ruby gently on the head. His expression told us that he understood that something was very, very wrong.

"I don't know . . . yet," answered Musetta. "But I'm beginning to think that maybe we're not so helpless, if we put our minds to it."

Gubbins began to tik and whir. We were desperate for ideas, so we all tried to be patient and listen. "Whir-tik-whir-tik," he said. "Tik-whir-tik-tik, whir-whir-whir, tik-tik-whir, whir-tik-tik, tik-tik-tik."

"Clouds," I translated. "Quite so—bad timing with a storm coming. It'll cover up a nice full moon."

Gubbins shook his head and continued, "Tik-tik-whir-tik, tik-whir-tik-tik, whir-tik-whir-whir."

"Fly?" inquired Musetta, glancing at me. "Clouds fly?"

Gubbins nodded vigorously.

We responded with blank stares.

"Er . . . quite," I said.

Musetta turned toward me and shrugged one shoulder and an eyebrow. On her way to collapse on the settee, she whispered, "Poor guy's blown a gasket."

Clouds fly. We might have expected such an inane comment from Rumple, if Rumple spoke, but not from Gubbins. Perhaps the stress really had thrown a wrench into his mechanized jumble.

Or perhaps our friend was several steps ahead of us all.

⋆　　⋆　　⋆

17

Where Humans Dare

Hours and hours had passed. We were beginning to fear that the Flying Fays had lost their quarry.

None of us had any idea how far away the Big City was. We knew that Father sometimes went there on business and returned late the next day. Given time for business, we figured the travel time couldn't take more than half a day each way. The Fays would cover the distance far quicker than a carriage ride, so . . .

Back to being disheartened.

I went downstairs to the drawing room to take my turn at listening for news. The room had lost its usual cheerful, homey feel. In his armchair by the unlit fireplace, Father leaned forward with his head in his hands. Serious men with serious whiskers came and went.

Dandie, as distraught as the people, curled up at Father's feet. I took a seat on the dog's shoulder and scratched him behind one ear, hoping to comfort him.

I had just settled in when a swooshing noise came from the fireplace. Dandie heard it, too; he lifted his head with such a start it almost threw me off.

In a blur of light unseen by human eyes, the Flying Fays swooped into the drawing room through the fireplace. They shot right past Dandie and me to the stairhall, flew over the staircase altogether, and swerved toward the nursery.

Dandie was hot on their trail at full velocity. After some ignoble bouncing around, I swung one leg over his back and made like a jockey. This was my first solo, high-speed Dinmont ride— exhilarating to say the least! My ears flapped like pennant flags as we careened out of the drawing room and through the stairhall, dashed up the stairway, and finished with a breakneck sprint to the nursery.

Poor Dandie would be deprived of his prey yet again, for the Fays had already zipped into the window-seat parlor. As my steed pulled to a frustrated stop, I dismounted with a leap and run that, if I say so myself, exhibited my athleticism at its best. Unfortunately, no one else was around to notice. Isn't that always the way.

Inside, I found the Twins already playing chase with the Fays. Pixies in the parlor—quite a novelty!

"They've found Bingo!" Musetta announced as I entered. "Just as we guessed: They took him to the Big City."

Gracie and Ruby squealed, "Eee!"

At the same time, the Fays confirmed our interpretation of their find by flying into a tizzy. Not ones for confined spaces, they shot out of the parlor without further delay.

"And we're going," Musetta added simply.

This seemed rash to me, given our materiality-deprived state. "You're not saying, to the B-I-G-C-I-T-Y?"

"That's right."

"The deuce you say!"

"I mean it, Thursby. We are nursery figments, after all."

"Quite so. Figments who live in the nursery."

"Figments who live there to take care of children! Besides, it's no different than you going to sea to help Great-grandfather! Or at least, trying to."

"And it was a silly thing to attempt. What's more, I was a baby myself! Why I'd only been imagined about a dozen years before."

"Aren't you the one who's always saying, 'Fine ears butter no parsnips'?"

"An apt proverb when it comes to collecting supplies, or preparing snacks, or rehearsing for a play. Cosy activities! A far cry from human affairs of life-and-death proportion!"

"Ah, bunk," said Musetta, hands on her hips. She turned and asked, "Gubbins, what do you say?"

We listened with bated breath.

"Tik-whir-whir, tik," he began. And then, continuing, "whir-whir-tik, whir-whir-whir."

I interpreted: "We go."

"We're going!" shouted Gracie. "Hooray!"

"Hooray!" yelled Ruby. "Here we go!" Then the girls looked at one another.

"Wait," said Gracie, starting the question—

"—where are we going?" asked Ruby, finishing it.

"The Big City, evidently," I explained.

"Eee!"

Musetta knelt down before them. "Girls, our sweet baby Bingo has been snatched. This very moment, he's all alone, probably crying himself to sleep. He might not have a window to see the Moon at night. He has no one to snuggle him or sing to him or—"

"Baaaahhhhh!" the Twins wailed with a full complement of tears. "We want to go! Poor little Bingo!"

"Very well," I said, surrendering. "Looks like we're outvoted, eh, Rumple?" Rumple had actually spent this time waving at his own shadow. On the other hand, he hadn't said that he did *not* agree with me.

I attempted to calm the Twins, and probably myself, too, by telling them, "The Big City might not be so scary as all that. We've probably built it up frightfully in our imaginations."

"Imaginations?" said Gracie, screwing up her face in confusion.

"Yes. We've probably imagined it to be more scary than it really is."

"But Cozies are imaginary, right?" asked Ruby.

"Well, yes, that's true."

The Twins exchanged looks. Gracie asked hesitantly, "So . . . imaginary beings have imaginations?"

"Um . . . " I looked at Musetta. She shrugged her patented shoulder-and-an-eyebrow shrug. " . . . evidently," I finished.

You may recognize here the genesis of the theory now known as *layered imaginations*. I have since referred to the concept regularly in my academic writings and, allegorically, in my poetry.

Thankfully, Dandie saved me trying to explain such a complex concept off the cuff. His snarfling and puffing snout suddenly pressed through the parlor entrance. Gubbins grabbed Pudding by the collar to hold her back.

Musetta stepped over and leaned against the hound's twitching black nose. "Now, then," she said, "anyone know where we can find a good Dinmont?"

⋆   ⋆   ⋆

18

The Dinmont Caravan

Conveyance by Dinmont, of course, was the obvious choice. Too obvious, perhaps: Had we opened the subject for discussion—had we used our imaginations, and specifically Gubbins' imagination, rather than rushing forward like a fullback at the goal line—we might have saved a full day. In our hurry, though, Musetta and I charged straight up the middle.

At our request, Gubbins took on the duty of Dinmont-caravan design. He modeled the caravan generally on the maharajah's elephant saddle on the big burgundy pillow in the nursery. Elephant saddles, it turns out, appear frequently in the dreams of children in elephant-riding regions. Gubbins retrieved an enchanting example from the world of dreams.

Sleigh-like, with two bench seats, the saddle impressed with its majesty. Pouncing lions with burnished-silver bodies and golden heads, manes, and paws framed the sides. Their tails curved along as armrests for the back seat. The footrest of the front seat rolled upward to provide a front dash—to keep excited young maharajahs from falling forward onto the elephant, I would think.

Soon we had outfitted the Dinmont with our picturesque perch, a canopy to ward off sun or rain, and side panels with ladders.

"We added the yellow fringe to the canopy," declared Gracie proudly.

Ruby held her hands up and wiggled her fingers. "Doesn't it look pretty swaying back and forth?" she asked. The Twins' little wings had hardly stopped fluttering since we decided to leave for the Big City.

"Gorgeous!" I agreed, tugging on the port-side ladder to test its stability.

Dandie turned his head and gave me a peeved look. He was *not* pleased with his accoutrement.

Ladies and Gentlemen, some of you might think that we took more time than necessary in preparation. Given the emergency, as it were. I offer two reasons for this, if not excuses: First, for Cozies to set aside our habit of leisurely preparation presented quite a challenge; that said, we did accelerate our usual pace.

Secondly, we were unsure what might happen once we entered the world beyond our family's estate. Although great advances have been made in the science of figmentology, many unknowns remain. That was even more true *au fin-de-siècle.*

Facing the unknown, then, required extra preparation. To cite the well-known saying: *It takes more than elegant ears to outrun a rhino.*

In any event, the expedition was soon ready. We mounted up. The Twins started off in their usual place in the tuft of fur on top of Dandie's head. Musetta had the front seat to herself for now, and Gubbins and I shared the backseat. For Rumple and our supplies, Gubbins had fashioned a sort of luggage rack that extended from the back of the elephant saddle and along Dandie's hindquarters. Rumple never minds the elements, you see. He possesses a distinct affinity for nature in all its forms—and vice versa.

The humans were so distracted that we probably could have trotted past under full moonlight—in other words, fully visible. In any event, no one appeared to notice as Dandie ambled through Father's study, across the piazza, and through the carriage port to the driveway.

The Flying Fays flew on ahead to the front gate. They alighted atop one of the gate posts and flashed like a beacon, summoning us to follow.

Dandie was unimpressed. Despite the beacon and our urging, his forward progress could only be described as meandering. Anything higher than a blade of grass presented a reason to stop, sniff, and mark. With each stop, our caravan would sway forward for the sniffing, and sideways for the marking. Stop, sniff, mark. Halt, forward, sideways. Et cetera.

We finally arrived at the front gate. Once there, Dandie plopped down on his behind. This position put us on an angle and left us pressed against our seat backs.

Gubbins dismounted. Like a good elephant driver, he attempted to push, tap, and pull the Dinmont off of his behind and out the gate.

"Whir-whir-tik! Whir-whir-whir," ordered Gubbins, telling Dandie simply *Go!* with a forceful emphasis on the tik. "Whir-whir-tik! Whir-whir-whir." And so forth, to no avail.

The Twins had soon had enough. Gracie stepped onto Dandie's snout and pulled on his frontal fur tuft, ordering him, "Come on! Come on, come on, come *onnnnnnn*!"

Ruby stepped the other way and pushed at the back of Dandie's head. "Go! Go, go, go-ohhhhh!"

Musetta joined in next. She climbed over the front dash and leaned toward one hanging ear. "Come on, sweetie," she wooed. "Go get Bingo. Go get Bingo!"

That captured Dandie's attention. The Dinmont caravan was off and running!

Charging out the front gate, scampering down the road, swimming across the canal, loping through the tall grass of the fields, making his way overland toward the Big City: Dandie clearly had no intention whatsoever of undertaking any of those activities.

Instead, Dandie ran straight back home. He must have believed that Bingo was back—after all Musetta had said so, hadn't she? The bullheaded terrier dashed back up the driveway, around to the side of the house to the carriage port, onto the piazza and around to the back of the house, into and through Father's study, and all the way upstairs to the nursery.

Right where we started.

★   ★   ★

19

Back to the Drawing Room

Musetta, the Twins, and I spent most of the first night after the baby-snatching along the window sill in the drawing room. We kept watch and prayed that the humans would find Bingo. Police and searchers arrived and departed from time to time even during the night.

Each approaching carriage teased us with the hope that they were bringing our boy home to us. Every time the bell on the new telephone rang, we nearly jumped out of our imaginary skin. We weren't used to that newfangled contraption.

We took turns checking on Mother upstairs. The Twins had gone last, coming back downstairs as a gray morning dawned.

"Mother keeps trying to get out of bed," Gracie told us.

"Bridie won't let her," added Ruby, pressing her face to the front window to look out.

"Because of Mother's tummy ache," theorized Gracie.

In the late evening, not long after the Dinmont-caravan attempt, Mother had been pacing in the drawing room, keeping watch. Suddenly she had clutched at her waist and moaned. You'll recall me mentioning that Mother had grown rather, um, bulbous, in the middle.

Right before our eyes she almost tumbled over, like some sort of bulbous-middled, falling person. Stumbling back, at the last second she had lowered herself into Father's chair.

"That's enough!" Bridie had announced. "Up to bed with you, this minute!"

Since then, the Twins had developed their own theories about Mother's health.

"Maybe her tummy got too big," Ruby said in earnest.

The twin *à gauche* nodded. "It's as big as a balloon." Gracie's big blue eyes widened. "And balloons pop!"

Ruby's and Gracie's mouths dropped open as they exchanged frightened looks.

I knelt beside the girls, giving them each a gentle, playful tug on the wings. "Girls, I promise you: Mother's tummy is not going to pop."

"Are you sure?" they asked, clinging to each other.

"Her tummy won't pop," Musetta said, still staring out the window, "but her heart might break. Poor girl. She wants to help, but can't—just like us. I've never wanted to be real, but now I'd give anything for it!"

"You two were gone a long time," I said, trying to distract the Twins. "Did you stop by the nursery?"

Gracie nodded. "Rumple is still in the crib."

"He still thinks he can find Bingo there," said Ruby.

"What about Gubbins? Still at his drafting table?"

"Uh-huh," confirmed Gracie. "He's drawing pictures of clouds!"

"Clouds with wings," said Ruby, giving a slightly confused smile.

Clouds with wings, I thought. I wonder . . .

At that moment, Dandie galloped into the room with what we would now call cinematic timing. Gubbins rode on his back. The truth is, Gubbins not only rode the Dinmont, but actually stood on Dandie's shoulders.

"Look at Gubbins!" cried Gracie.

"He's like a trick rider in a Wild West show!" cheered Ruby.

Even Musetta—not easily impressed by *les activités sportives*—professed, "Quite the swashbuckler!"

I must confess: The swashbuckling entry aroused in me a bit of the green-eyed monster. After all, my leaping arrival the day before had gone unseen by anyone. I tried my best to be sporting. "Not bad," was the best I could muster.

Ticking and whirring for all he was worth, Gubbins waved at us to come with him. We didn't wait for the words—obviously something was up. He lined Dandie up below us, and we jumped down onto the terrier's back.

Gubbins sat down for a less showy ride up to the nursery.

*   *   *

20

Clouds Fly

On Dandie's approach to the window seat, I made the rather poor decision of attempting my dashing leap-and-run again. Riding on the dog's back between Musetta and Rumple, though, left me with little room to maneuver. That resulted in . . . well, let's simply say that Rumple and I did some nasty bouncing along on the floor. No need to dwell on it.

Once inside the parlor, Gubbins directed us to take seats in front of his drafting table, which was tilted up for display and covered with a blank sheet.

The Twins exchanged looks of scrunched-face confusion.

"Is he going to show us a picture?" asked Gracie.

"That would be silly," responded Ruby. "It's not the second Tuesday of the month!"

Musetta and I also exchanged glances. Not only was it not the assigned day of the month for artistic presentations, there were far more important things on our minds.

"He's lost it," whispered Musetta.

I wasn't so sure. The rest of us did not have Gubbins' mechanical imagination. I was about to be proven right. About Gubbins' rightness, that is.

Gubbins started talking. As I've mentioned, his method of speech can turn even a brief description into a lengthy one. Nevertheless, our fellow Cozy's ticks and whirs held us spellbound.

For our purposes today, I will condense Gubbins' explanation. In fact, I will reduce it to two short words: "Whir-tik-whir-tik, tik-whir-tik-tik, whir-whir-whir, tik-tik-whir, whir-tik-tik, tik-tik-tik—tik-tik-whir-tik, tik-whir-tik-tik, whir-tik-whir-whir."

In other words: *Clouds fly.*

With admirable flourish, Gubbins threw back the cover from his display.

"Oooooooo," we breathed, followed by uniform applause. Uniform, that is, except for Rumple. He looked back and forth between us and a step-by-step diagram of Gubbins' ingenious plan to convey us to the Big City, *sans*-Dinmont.

As soon as the rest of us stopped applauding, Rumple started. Then he noticed that we were all staring at him. His clapping slowed like a mechanical monkey winding down to a stop.

You see, the most prominent figure in Gubbins' diagram was . . . Rumple himself.

Next exhibit, please.

(Flip-chart Exhibit #5: "Detail From the 'Clouds Fly' Diagram—Airborne Rumple")

EXHIBIT #5

RUMPLE

*   *   *

21

To Catch a Cloud

By mid-afternoon, the clouds we needed finally arrived—white and fluffy, and enough of them to raise our chances of capturing one. You heard me correctly, my friends: The first step in our redesigned mission was *to catch a cloud*.

I can guess what you're thinking: How is that possible, Thursby old chap? Assuming a Cozy could even reach a cloud, how could said Cozy do anything with it?

As to reaching the clouds, that issue will be addressed presently. As to Cozy-cloud interaction, you might be forgetting a basic precept from your elementary education: Clouds are the stuff that dreams are made of.

(The speaker pauses, looking at the audience expectantly.)

Hm? That concept is taught in human schools, is it not? No? Perhaps we need to contact Mr. Clarence Darrow to see about correcting that omission! Ha, ha. I'm joking, of course.

In any event, as the stuff that dreams are made of, clouds can be touched, moved, molded, and otherwise manipulated, so to speak, by Cozies.

Which brings us to the problem of access. How would a small party of diminutive, imaginary beings reach a substance thousands of feet overhead?

Sounds impossible, yet Gubbins had developed a plan.

This morning, if you recall, I made a passing reference to tugboat winches. Surprisingly, tugboats appear regularly in children's dreams. One doesn't have to be Doctor Freud to understand the appeal for children of small but powerful boats that lead larger ships around by the end of a rope.

Tugboat winches, on the other hand, are more rare. Children often dream in broad outlines. Sometimes merely the general shape of a dreamed thing will appear in the *Traumwelt*. Only the most astute child tugboat enthusiast will include a detail like a functioning winch for a vessel splashing over the blue-green waves of the Sea of Dreams.

Just the same, Gubbins, our scavenger extraordinaire, had found a functioning tugboat winch. A basic model, the winch was simply a rotating drum on its side, mounted on a circular platform with a twine-like rope spooled around it. Attached to one bright-yellow end panel was a hand crank. The crank turned the drum to extend or retract the rope.

At our sky-gazing spot on the roof, Gubbins affixed the tugboat winch to the rooftop shingles. Some last minute adjustments were needed—never a problem for Gubbins. If some bolt, spring, or sprocket comes up missing in a project, Gubbins can usually find it somewhere on his person—and I mean literally on his person.

The billowing landscapes high above mesmerized Rumple. Cloud watching always put him into a sort of trance. Probably best—that way he didn't notice when we attached him to the other end of the winch rope.

"Fluffy white clouds!" announced the Twins with fluttering wings. "Coming this way!"

I did a quick comparison with Gubbins' diagram. "Perfect! They should be overhead soon. Everyone ready?"

"Whir-tik-whir-whirrrrr!" sounded Gubbins.

"Ready here!" reported Musetta, in charge of Rumple-readiness. She tugged on the front of Rumple's flight harness, where the winch-rope was tied. Attached to the back of the harness was a bright yellow knapsack with dark blue trim. Protruding from the top of the knapsack was a hook like the end of a shepherd's crook. At the base of the knapsack was a ring like those used by acrobats.

"Ready!" announced the twin on the right. Ruby held up the Rumple-inflation device—our fireplace bellows, inflated fully with hot air.

"Ready!" confirmed the twin *à gauche*. Gracie stood by with the sealant, a gummy concoction known as plum glue. Plum glue is made from sugar plums, visions of which, as you may know, tend to dance in children's heads.

Last but certainly not least, the Flying Fays signaled their readiness by swooshing around Rumple, and back into the sky above.

"Right, then," I said. "On my signal."

We waited with bated breath for our target nebulosity to drift overhead. A storm was on its way. If we missed this flock of fluffy whites, we might have to wait days to try again. Days that could mean all the difference for Bingo.

"Now!" I yelled. "Launch!"

Ruby passed the Rumple-inflation device to Musetta. Musetta stuck the tip of the bellows into Rumple's mouth. Even this didn't rouse him from his cloud trance until she gave the device a squeeze, forcing hot air into him.

Rumple crossed his eyes quizzically at the bellows sticking out of his mouth. Fortunately, with Rumple you can pretty much count on a delay factor, even for basic decisions. And you can't get much more basic than whether or not to exhale.

Still, Musetta had to act quickly. She tossed the bellows to Ruby on the right, grabbed the twin on the left, lifted her up, and Gracie smeared a slathering of sealant onto Rumple's lips.

Rumple floated upward.

★   ★   ★

22

A Rumplish Paradise

Gubbins had figured the physics flawlessly. The response of Rumple was another matter.

Not that the sudden sensation of floating phased our elemental friend. His elephant-foot-like feet paddled uselessly at first, as if we were the ones leaving and he was simply going to waddle along after us. When he sensed that he was not making headway, he waved bye-bye.

At that point, the Flying Fays swirled in front of Rumple's face and upward. Rumple's gaze followed them; once he saw that he was getting closer to the fascinating fluffiness in the sky, he never looked back. Overhead flew a flock of clouds of all sizes.

Up, up, and further up flew our friend!

The blues and whites in the sky began to camouflage Rumple's translucent, baby-blue body. Soon he faded from sight altogether. All we could see was the rope, extending up thousands of feet and disappearing far overhead. Occasionally we spotted a tiny shimmering that we figured were the Fays.

"They're so high up!" observed Gracie.

"I can't even see them anymore," said Ruby, giving a palms-up shrug.

"Gubby," Musetta said, "I understand the sealant on Rumple's lips, but what's to keep him from exhaling through his nose?"

Gubbins jerked his head suddenly to look at Musetta. His hairspring eye contracted tightly, his telescope eye withdrew. His head started twitching to one side.

"Eee!" squealed the Twins.

Uh-oh, I thought. Apparently Gubbins had missed that one possibility in his plan.

Musetta tried to calm everyone. "He hasn't thought of it so far. Let's keep our fingers crossed."

Gracie and Ruby each instantly held up both hands with their little fingers crossed for good luck.

Later, the Flying Fays would relate the adventure to us through pantomime. I call this peculiar skill *flight mime*. First the Fays would zip back and forth as white lights to perform their own role, then they'd unite as an oval of blue lights to represent Rumple.

They would show us that the next step in the cloud-catching plan went well. When Rumple arrived at the correct height, the Fays, like a tugboat in the sky, pulled Rumple sideways to get him near one of the passing clouds.

The mistiness of the cloud edges melted the plum-glue on Rumple's lips. By the time he floated above the clouds, Rumple's mouth popped open and the hot air from the fireplace bellows escaped.

> (Here the speaker makes a lip-flapping sound, which the transcriber shall report as "Pll-ip-p-p-p-p-p-p . . . .")

"Pll-ip-p-p-p-p-p-p . . . ," and so forth.

(Here, again, a brief pause for cleaning of the transcriber's spectacles is required.)

Ahem. My apologies.

The escaping hot air shot Rumple out over the nearest cloud. He came down hard, bouncing along on top of the cloud. Of course, coming down hard onto the soft, springy surface of a cloud is really quite nice.

Rumple sat up, licking away the remaining plum glue. He looked around at the soft, rolling cloudscape. In the distance, more clouds drifted alongside as dreamily as sailboats on a calm lake.

A look came into Rumple's eyes, the look of someone who has *arrived*. This was heaven. He had floated up to a rumplish paradise.

Rumple scooped up an armful of cloud and hugged it, then another and another. He jumped to his feet and twirled around, blowing kisses at the soft, curvy, gentle vista.

The Flying Fays saw that our mission was in jeopardy. They swirled around Rumple, trying to distract him. Somehow they had to get him to a smaller cloud—small enough for us to lower to Earth. The seven Fays arranged themselves as a flashing arrow. They zigzagged in front of Rumple's dazed and giddy face. They swirled and pounded and pantomimed. Nothing worked.

Rumple started to dance across the cloudscape, springing like a ballet dancer from one fluffy knoll to the next. With the blues of the sky and whites of the clouds reflecting through his round, billowy body, he looked almost like a cloud himself. A little elephantine cloud, suddenly as graceful as a hippopotamus dropping into water.

Rumple neared the cloud's edge. The Fays saw that he had no intention of stopping his happy, prancing dance—his distraction spelled doom. Yet when he hit the edge, Rumple performed a sort of *grand jeté en avant*. His goal: a much smaller cloud poised like an island between larger cloudscapes.

Rumple landed on the small cloud and romped on across. The Fays saw their chance. They snatched the hook at the top of his knapsack and carried it through the air in the other direction. This extracted from the knapsack a giant, silky sheet, dark blue with bright yellow stars. The fluttering sheet unfurled behind Rumple like a cape. It billowed out and grew longer and wider as the light-sprites flew.

Where, you might ask, would such a specialized item as this star-spangled sheet come from? The answer is simple: What dream is complete without a starry-night background? The ever-ingenious Gubbins had shaved a sheet-thin slice of starry night from the world of children's dreams. He attached one end of the sheet to the inside of Rumple's knapsack, and folded the rest into it, just so.

As the Fays dove over the small cloud's rim behind him, Rumple performed a second *grand jeté* off of the far side—meant to carry him to the next big cloud. But the starry-night sheet, which as I said was attached firmly to his knapsack, caught him up short.

I believe we have a schematic?

(Flip-chart Exhibit #6: "Cloud Capture Diagram")

From there, mid-leap, Rumple found himself dropping between the clouds.

*   *   *

2 3

Nabbing Nebuli

Do not fear, Ladies and Gentlemen. Rumple did not fall to his . . . whatever happens to imaginary beings who fall from great heights.

Because the knapsack was secured to Rumple, and one end of the starry-night sheet was attached to the knapsack, Rumple dropped only a short distance before swinging beneath the small cloud.

There beneath the small cloud, the Fays flew toward Rumple from the other direction. As they flew, the starry-night sheet billowed out to the sides, encompassing the cloud.

Rumple saw the Flying Fays shooting toward him. Untroubled as always, he waved hello.

Too busy at the moment to pause for polite greetings, the Fays flew past Rumple's head and over his back to—juuuuuust *barely*—attach the hook on their end of the sheet to the ring extending from the bottom of Rumple's knapsack. The nebulous fluff was fully enfolded.

In other words, the cloud was caught.

The Fays flew down close enough for us to see them. They glowed brighter three times. This signaled us to start reeling in the rope.

By this time, the clouds had moved on a ways. The rope extended over and beyond the next-door pasture. Our catch emerged from the distance, lowering to us like a kite being pulled home.

"There it is!" yelled Musetta. She knelt down beside the Twins and pointed.

"Hooray!" cried the girls, fluttering their little wings so hard they almost lifted off of the rooftop.

"They did it!" I shouted. And to Gubbins, "*You* did it, old bean!"

"Coo-coo! Coo-coo!" coo-cooed Gubbins.

The captured cloud drew closer until we could make out the colors of its night-of-dreams wrapping—darkest blue, like night, with bright yellow stars.

"Oooooo," said the Twins together, "it's pretty!"

Then, finally, we could make out Rumple, hanging below the starry-night-wrapped cloud. Despite the winch-to-Rumple rope extending from his waist, he appeared comfortable enough. He gazed tranquilly around at the scenery. You would never guess he was returning from a potentially dangerous adventure at dizzying heights.

When Rumple spotted us, he applauded—a simple gesture that made us all feel good about ourselves. Nothing boosts the spirit like a genuinely happy greeting.

And we all needed spirit boosting. Our quest was only beginning.

$\star$ $\star$ $\star$

24

The Airship Starry Night

Icould tell by the look on some of your faces that you have guessed the goal of Gubbins' cloud-catching plan. Yes, we were going by airship, or perhaps most accurately, a blimp. In these halcyon days after Mr. Lindbergh's brave crossing, the idea of flight might not strike one as ingenious—but Gubbins' idea of creating our own airship was purely that.

Now that we had the cloud, we proceeded to mold the nebulous material into a more aerodynamic shape. Next we sewed the starry-night sheet so that it fit snugly around our newly acquired nebulosity.

Our sky whale also needed fins to swim smoothly through the air. Musetta and I affixed flat flippers known as rudders and elevators to the airship's back end. The rudders would guide it from side to side, the elevators up and down.

To hang underneath the cloud-blimp and convey us through the sky, Gubbins adapted the maharajah's elephant saddle and the Rumple-and-luggage rack as our gondola. Behind that was the engine. The engine consisted of a propeller powered by a bicycle-like contraption that people used to call a velocipede.

By sunset the airship was ready.

(Flip-chart Exhibit #7: "The Airship Starry Night")

EXHIBIT #7

A sight to behold, *n'est-ce pas?*

We gathered for a brief ceremonial moment. Musetta approached the vessel with a hefty bottle of sparkling cider in hand.

"I dub thee, *Starry Night!*" she announced. She smashed the bottle against the airship's nose.

The subsequent repairs only took about fifteen minutes.

"Cast off!"

At Musetta's command, I released the moorings and jumped aboard. The *Starry Night* lifted away from the rooftop.

The Twins were seated on the front bench of the elephant saddle, and I joined Musetta on the second seat. Rumple sat behind us on the luggage rack; our miscellaneous supplies provided a backrest for him. Behind the supplies was the tugboat winch. Gubbins, furthest back on the retrofitted velocipede, started pedaling, which turned the gears that spun the propeller.

"It's working!" cried the Twins.

"By George, you've done it again, Gubbins!" I called toward the back.

The Flying Fays took off from their perch on the chimney. They swirled around us in a broad circle. Then they zipped to the south, or perhaps it was the north, but it was distinctly not toward the sunset, which was in front of us. Gubbins turned a tiller, in front of him, to control the rudders. We gradually shifted directions by ninety degrees. Silhouetted by the sunset, the *Starry Night* followed the Fays' seven tiny beacons.

The Twins were standing and looking over the front dash of the elephant-saddle-gondola.

"Look, there's Hazel in the pasture," said Gracie, pointing.

Ruby stuck her tongue out at the sneering milk cow. "Nyyyyaaaa!"

"Girls, please stay in your seats" said Musetta. "I'm afraid you're going to—oh my gosh! Everything's getting so small!" Musetta jumped to her feet and leaned half out of the gondola. "I feel like a giant!"

PART FOUR

Into the Lair of the Louts

25

Quietly Through the Heavens

(The speaker pauses to signal the passage of time.
He nods to his assistant. Flip-chart Exhibit #8:
"The Moon with Smiling Eyes.")

EXHIBIT #8

"Hello, Moon!" called Gracie to the brilliant orb, who had risen up to watch over us.

"Hello, Moon!" called Ruby.

The girls were back with Rumple, sitting on the supplies near his head. They enjoyed the best view all around from there.

Musetta had climbed forward onto the front seat of the elephant saddle; she and I were both stretched out across our own seating. The ride was spectacular.

Only the gentle *woosh, woosh, woosh* of the propeller broke the silence. Our friend the Moon watched over us, big and bright in the sky. The twinkling lights of farmhouses and villages speckled the moonlit pastures below. Bingo's welfare weighed on us no less than before. Moving so quietly through the heavens, though, we all felt as if everything would turn out all right.

Little did we know, this was only the calm before the storm—figuratively and literally.

The trip was shorter than expected. Seeing the vast expanse of fields and streams and roads below, I began to appreciate Dandie's wisdom. The journey would have been grueling by Dinmont. But as the crow flies, or the blimp, the Big City wasn't so far away.

"Have you noticed the lights?" Musetta asked, looking down.

"More and more of them," I said.

"The brighter it gets down there, the fewer stars shine above."

"We must be getting close." I sat up straight, smoothed my ears, and straightened my vest and jacket. "Look ahead—due south. Or north."

Musetta faced forward and peered at the glowing horizon. "The Big City," she whispered.

At that moment, flickering lights in the sky revealed that dark storm clouds loomed.

"That's not good," commented Musetta.

"No," I agreed. "Without moonlight, I can't imagine how we'll notify the police."

"What are you two talking about?" demanded Gracie from back behind us. The Twins did not like to be left out of conversations.

"Yeah, what're you talking about?" repeated Ruby.

Rumple started to applaud and the girls followed his gaze ahead. Instantly the Twins crawled forward over Rumple to the back of the elephant saddle. I lifted them forward onto the front seat so that one stood on each side of Musetta.

"Is that it?" they asked Musetta, huddling against her.

"Yes, girls."

"Everything will be all right," said Gracie, to herself more than anything.

"We're going to save Bingo," said Ruby.

For a time we were all silent. We watched the Big City's glow grow on the horizon, and the crackling illuminations in the dark clouds ahead. The edges of the thunder clouds reached toward us like charcoal-colored claws.

*   *   *

26

An <u>Albtraumwelt</u>-like Vicinity

When some upcoming event frightens us—and by *us*, here I mean you and me and any thinking beings—we picture what it will be like. We imagine the possible scenarios, best and worst. While this can help us make plans, it can also scare us.

When the frightening event is no longer upcoming but is right here and now, our minds play an interesting trick: They make it seem like we are only imagining it all. *This can't be happening*, we say to ourselves.

If I might be so bold to suggest, the best thing to do at such times is to go with it. Pretend that you are simply pretending. The world is your stage, as the Bard said. Remember that *you* get to choose which character you want to play.

You may be thinking, Oh, Thursby—*quelle idée!* Pretense is fine in its place, but as the saying goes: *Pinned-down ears don't a lop-eared make.*

Yet I stand by my claim. Follow your dream, and you might find that the *you* you dream *is* you.

Besides, what's the option? Curl into a ball and suck your thumb? Well, yes, that is an option. But I knew a fellow named Leopold who made a very conscious decision to do exactly that, and he never felt very good about himself afterward.

I mention this fear-facing theory of mine because that weird sense of unreality fell over us as we arrived at the Big City—and by *us*, here I mean, well . . . me. By the time the *Starry Night* flew high over that sea of lights, our comforting friend, the Moon, had disappeared behind the storm. There we were, six nursery figments from a grand house in the country, arriving in a blimp at a frighteningly immense and noisy metropolis.

All the same, the strange beauty of that mad maze of light, sound, and motion transfixed us as we floated overhead.

As we neared the urban center, the Flying Fays guided us gradually lower. Though still at a considerable height, we could see people laughing and talking as their elegant carriages passed beneath gaslit street lamps. Men in top hats and women in shimmering dresses hurried on broad, clean sidewalks—trying to beat the storm to wherever they were going.

"Look!" cried Gracie, pointing.

"A horseless carriage!" declared Ruby.

Snicker if you must, but the automobile was a new invention in those days. Only vehicles powered by horse or human had ever come up the driveway of our grand house back up north. Or down south.

"How does it go?" asked Gracie.

"Is the man pedaling it?" asked Ruby.

"No," I answered, "it has what they call an internal combustion engine. It's, um, too complex to go into now."

We entered the business district. With menacing storm clouds as a backdrop, our airship slipped by skyscrapers like a fish from the open sea moving warily through a coral reef.

The downtown skyscrapers gave way to shorter buildings. The Fays guided us lower still. Soon we were only a stone's throw above the rooftops.

The city of top hats and fancy carriages disappeared, replaced by one of rags and pushcarts. Towers gave way to tenements. Pride to poverty. Of all the words used to describe the Big City, it seemed, missing was the word *sad*.

Then came the city's heart of darkness—a district of depravation so tawdry that even the poor refused to live there. This was a demesne of shadows and wraiths. Haggard women with angry eyes loitered below street lamps despite the weather. Scraggy men scurried through the gloom with sly, darting glances.

It felt as if we had crossed into the world of nightmares: the *Albtraumwelt*.

*   *   *

27

Courting Danger

"It's scary here," said Gracie.

Ruby jerked her head to look at me in the back seat. Wide-eyed, as if reading my mind she asked, "Are we in . . . Are we in . . . ?" She couldn't bring herself to say it.

I shook my head. "No, dear. We're not in the *Albtraumwelt*. Not that I'm so sure the real world is much better hereabouts."

Finally the Fays came to a stop above a dingy alleyway. They formed a flashing red arrow pointing downward.

"Looks like this is it," said Musetta.

"Eee!" squealed you-know-who.

"Pull up here, Gubbins!" I called toward the back.

Gubbins stopped pedaling, and our airship drifted to a stop over the alleyway.

The Fays flew down and swirled in loops around a third-story window, as if drawing a circle around it. Light glowed dimly from within.

Musetta noticed, "The window is open!"

"You're right," I said. "Only four or five inches, but I *might* be able to squeeze through."

"Why, Thursby!" smiled Musetta. "Humor in the face of danger. I'm impressed!"

My sleek black fur puffed up considerably. Complements from Musetta always have that effect on me.

We had decided earlier that I would go down first to confirm that we were in the right place. We moved back beside the tugboat winch to get ready.

The Twins fished a mountaineering harness out of our supplies. Musetta attached the end of our tugboat-winch rope to the harness. Next the Twins presented me with a mountaineering stake, yet another handy item procured by Gubbins. Thank goodness for children's dreams of adventure!

I slipped the stake into an inner pocket in my smart-yet-functional jacket. Musetta held the harness while I stepped into it.

"One moment, please," I requested. I smoothed my ears, straightened my vest, and made sure my jacket was hanging appropriately. Like a potential spouse, Danger should be courted with dignity.

I nodded. "All set." With my umbrella in one hand, the other holding the rope, I slipped over the side.

"Good luck, *old chum*," said Musetta, tossing off one of my own Briticisms with a wry smile.

"Be careful, Thursby," said each of the Twins as Gubbins cranked the tugboat winch, lowering me.

"Cheerio!" I called, more cheerily than I felt.

My friends were waving—all with worried expressions, even Rumple. Gubbins' eyes were adjusting to watch my descent. Beyond my fellow Cozies' worried faces was the star-spangled blimp, and beyond that the storm's restless rendering of charcoal grays.

The Fays buzzed around me excitedly as I descended from the airship. The wind swung me this way and that until I passed the tenement rooftop.

The shadows of the alley swallowed me up. A damp sheen clung to the brick wall. It was as if I were being lowered into a well. No, wait . . . into the maw of some monstrous beast!

(The speaker jots down a note.)

Yes, that's better: *maw . . . beast.*

I came to the window. Accumulated dust and grime on the glass obscured the view, but a lamp or candle was definitely burning within.

Chipped paint and decaying wood crunched under my feet on the window sill. Pulling the mountaineering stake from my jacket pocket, I affixed the rope to one of the few spots on the sill that was not falling apart completely.

The window opening was conveniently Cozy-sized, as we'd thought.

I peeked in.

*   *   *

28

Tik-whirrrrrrrr

I spotted Bingo immediately. They had a crib for him, which surprised me. He had pulled himself up to a standing position and was crying softly for "Momma." He was obviously distraught, overtired, and, in short, tear-streaked and pitiful.

No one else was in the room.

I turned to give the rope three pulls—our prearranged signal that we were in the right place. But when I turned, I bumped right into Gubbins. The Fays, I would learn, had given the rope the needed tugs immediately on my landing. They were a might peeved that we'd felt the need to confirm anything.

Coming off of the rope was Musetta, with the Twins right behind her. Rumple remained on the airship. Perhaps he thought he was up in the clouds again and wanted to stay there this time.

"Tik-whirrrrrrrr," said Gubbins, with the growly *whirrrrrrrr* falling away at the end.

I spun around. Sure enough: Gubbins had spotted Agnes, nanny *à la* kidnapper, entering the room. She approached Bingo, but the boy didn't reach out for her. Instead he burst full-on into tears, this time *screaming* "Mommaaaaaa!"

"Here's Momma," said Agnes as she lifted the screaming boy from the crib. His crying increased.

I was incredulous. "Either Agnes doesn't understand that Bingo is calling for his real mother—"

Musetta finished my thought: "Or she's trying to teach him to think of *her* as his mother!"

"Which means she's planning to keep him!"

From outside the room but not far off, a man's voice boomed, "Shut that brat up!"

"Why that—" started Musetta angrily. "Was that the brutish lout?"

"Not the same one as before," I replied. "We may have discovered a nest of them."

"*Eee*," squeaked the Twins quietly. They were hugging each other tightly. Looking up at the clouds, Gracie asked, "What do we do? Without the Moon, we can't talk to people, can we?"

"We can't do anything without moonlight!" cried Ruby.

Musetta countered firmly, "Yes we can. We can *learn* things. That way, we'll know what to do if we get an opportunity. No one wants to end up with our mouths hanging open with nothing to say, do they?"

Our mouths hanging open with nothing to say, we all shook our heads vigorously.

Musetta stepped inside to the interior sill. "No. Now let's go!"

We followed Musetta inside.

The room was lit only by a paraffin lamp, but that was enough. Stained, outmoded wallpaper hung in peeling strands. Wires dangled from remnants of a picture strip. Dust covered the floor so thickly that it puffed around the hem of Agnes's dress as she carried Bingo in circles in the room, trying to comfort him.

At least, I admitted to myself, Agnes is *trying* to comfort Bingo.

The Flying Fays hovered outside the window, watching, just like back home. I didn't know it then, but their habits were part of a special calling. Soon the Fays and their secret mission would make all the difference.

*   *   *

29

A Brute, a Fiend, and a Toady

Directly below the interior window sill, an old radiator confirmed my belief that the decrepit building had known far better days. Vine patterns rose up on the radiator's iron folds like a bas-relief sculpture—the original occupants had clearly been people with taste. That refinement did not, however, extend to the current residents.

The five of us crawled off of the sill to the radiator. Holding our eyes and mouths closed, we slipped through accumulated dust and bug webs between the radiator folds, and down to the equally grimy, rugless floorboards.

At the base of the radiator we met with a mouse. On seeing five doubtlessly strange-looking beings drop into its own shadowy space, the mouse froze much like Pudding had at the crux of the Dandie-Pudding Incident.

Now, one look at this mouse of the louts' house would tell most anyone that it was not to be trifled with. Unlike well-groomed Pudding back home, this oily and malodorous creature had *Do Not Touch* written all over it—figuratively speaking, of course. Gubbins' soft spot for animals, however, clouded his judgment. He went right up and attempted to scratch the poor thing behind the ears.

> *(Here the speaker makes a loud and—if the transcriber might be permitted to editorialize—somewhat excessive screeching sound, which the transcriber will indicate simply as "Screeeeech!")*

"Screeeeech!" screeched the mouse with a shriek more like a bat's call than a sound expected from a mouse, wild or domesticated. The beast followed this up with a swipe at Gubbins with yellow fangs sharp as needles. Suffice it to say that I actually felt sorry for the creature at the sound of his fangs crunching against Gubbins' metallic arm.

The putrid rodent scurried away and slipped through a gap between the floorboards and the radiator pipe.

"Makes you appreciate Pudding, doesn't it," I said to Gubbins.

"*Pa-ding!*" he chimed wistfully.

"C'mon," said Musetta. "I want to see who else is here."

With Musetta in the lead, we ran near the baseboards toward the door. Bingo spotted us, which was good, because it distracted him from his plight for a moment.

"Hey!" the child said, putting his crying jag on hold. He pointed toward us. "D'go coozies!"

Agnes didn't even glance in our direction. "Mousey?" she asked. "Did Bingo see a mousey?"

We left the makeshift nursery, but we didn't have to do much exploring. The flat only contained one other room, which appeared to serve multiple purposes: drawing room, dining room, and kitchen. Please note that I'm the first one to champion the advantages of compact size. *Snug*, however, loses its charm when coupled with *squalid*.

Come to think of it, any word loses its charm when coupled with *squalid*.

Of course, a floor-level point of view often reveals forgotten nooks and crannies that collect dust. In the kidnappers' multipurpose room, though, the dust had collected long enough to become an oily sort of grime. This concoction filled the nooks and crannies like little snow drifts.

Various insects traveled to and from their homes within a home.

A three-legged table rested its legless corner on a shelf in a shallow, doorless cupboard. Sitting at the table were two male louts, playing cards.

One behind the other, the five of us helped each other up the cupboard shelves to the table top; there we had a better view of our adversaries. 'Twas not a pretty sight.

Sitting to our right, with his back to the makeshift nursery and facing the closed entry door was none other than the chief kidnapper—the sneering, brutish lout who had snatched Bingo through the nursery window.

Across from the brutish lout was another, whom I would describe as more *sinister* than brutish. From the pointy widow's peak of his hair, which began right above the eyebrows, his head sloped upward sharply. A lack of earlobes at the base of small but pointy ears only added to the sharpness of his features.

As a rule one would feel sorry for the owner of such odd features. But just as the assault on Gubbins had dampened our compassion for the house mouse, the sinisterness of the second lout thwarted any sympathy. At first glance one suspected his fiendishness. Further observation only confirmed it.

He gazed at the world by tilting his head forward and squinting slyly upward. He smiled frequently, but only at the possibility of violence or trouble for someone else, or—as the Twins noticed later—when he won at cards.

"Come on, Tim," said the sinister lout to the brutish. "Go fish."

"Tim?!" we all chimed at once, including Gubbins, who sounded a literal chime of surprise.

"Not *Dagger*?" offered Musetta.

"Or *Blackjack*?" I suggested.

Gracie giggled. "Or maybe . . . *Sneery*," she proposed.

Not to be outdone, Ruby announced, "I'd call him, um, *McUgly*."

The Twins simultaneously turned toward one another, their round little mouths popped open, and they exclaimed: "Sneery McUgly!" This launched the duo into the beginnings of a giggle fit, but the interlude was cut short—

With surprising speed, the brutish lout, also known as Tim, alias Sneery McUgly, looked right in our direction and lifted up an old shoe, heel down, as if he were going to strike us with it.

"Aaaaaaa!" we yelled, not accustomed to being spotted . . . or squashed with a shoe, for that matter.

Tim paused. With his trademark sneer in full bloom, he squinted, surveying the corner of the table top where we huddled.

"Swore I saw a roach," said Tim, slowly lowering his footwear weapon.

Only then did we notice: Here and there on the table top, camouflaged among cigar butts and burns, food scraps, and stains, were the squashed remains of more than a few cockroaches.

"Aaaaaaa!" we yelled again, not accustomed to finding ourselves in the middle of a roach killing field.

Our shout was followed by silence. Tim and the sinister, as-yet-unnamed lout turned their suspicious gazes toward the entry door. Then we heard it—footsteps mounting a stairway. Tim sneered. The sinister lout drew a knife from under his ratty jacket. The polished steel of the knife blade glinted in the lamplight.

"Well!" I commented. "At least they keep *something* clean around here."

"Shhh," said Musetta. "Someone's coming."

★   ★   ★

30

A Horrific Gesture

The doorknob turned. I made a mental note that the door was not locked. The door swung open and a large man entered and quickly shut the door behind him.

"Hi, Dave. Hi, Tim," said the man with a nod at each of the louts.

The man was so tall he'd ducked coming through the doorway, and so broad he'd turned slightly sideways to fit through. Yet his presence impressed one with a general sense of softness. Physically, I think, he was the kind of man Rumple might have been were Rumple human. Except, of course, a human Rumple would never be mixed up in a fiendish plot.

The sinister lout flicked his knife showily in the air. "I told you, Larry, it's not 'Dave' anymore. It's 'Maggot.' S'what all the boys in the pen called me."

Musetta and I looked at each other. "'Maggot?'" I asked rhetorically. "He prefers 'Maggot'?"

"High aspirations," said Musetta with a roll of her eyes. "His mother must be *so* proud."

"Sorry, Dave," said the big soft man known as Larry. "I mean, Maggot."

"You make the call?" Tim asked Larry.

"Yeah. Boy, that was tougher than I reckoned."

"Talk to the lady?"

Larry paused, looked at the grimy floor, and shook his head quickly enough to jiggle his ruddy cheeks. "No, the husband. He said—"

"I told you to talk to the lady!" hollered Tim.

The sinister lout, whose name was Dave, evidently, but whom I shall refer to as Maggot in deference to his wishes, slipped his clean dagger back under his jacket. "Knew we shouldn't'a trusted him with the call," he said, his lips peeling into a grin of delight over Larry's failure.

"See," said Larry softly while blushing, "here's the thing: The husband said his wife was sick in bed. On account a' her kid gettin' kidnapped and all."

"So what?!" demanded Tim.

Larry lowered his head even more. "So . . . she couldn't come to the telephone."

"Idiot! Awright, so what did the husband say? They gonna play ball?"

"Yep!" said Larry, lifting his head and nodding quickly. "He's gonna leave the money like I told 'im. An'—just like you said, Tim—he tried to get us to give up the kid at the same time. Just like you said!"

"You better tell me you didn't agree to that."

"No, Tim, I didn't. I held firm on that one. Told him, no police or nothin', not if they wanna see the kid again."

"Awright. Good enough. Now all we gotta do is wait 'til mornin'."

Maggot leaned back in his chair. "An' it's easy street fer us from then on. First thing I'm'anna do is get myself a new knife— the biggest Bowie knife they got!"

"Again with the high aspirations," I remarked.

Larry interjected, "Oh, and I told the husband they'd get the kid back later in the day. But I wouldn't tell him when or where, no matter how much he asked!"

Maggot's lips peeled into another grin. "Yeah, they'll get the kid back—can't promise in what condition, though." He followed this with a high-pitched, nasally snickering that made his nostrils flare.

The snickering only confirmed our already low opinion of Mr. Maggot. A dishonest or malevolent laugh is always a giveaway for the soul within. As they say, *Beware of those whose ears don't jiggle when they giggle.*

The threatening intimation of Maggot's comment brought an approving sneer from Tim, but not Larry. The large man furrowed his brow and sat down at the table.

"Look here," he said, "you're not thinkin' a' hurtin' that little boy? I never signed on for that!"

"You stupid as you look?" asked Maggot, looking quite stupid himself, as people who say such things usually do. "There ain't no way that kid's goin' home. Right, Tim?"

"No way no how," Tim confirmed. "Too risky."

"The baby's stayin' with me!" declared Agnes from the doorway to the makeshift nursery. "That was the deal, right? If I helped, you wouldn't hurt the baby!"

Tim and Maggot stared at each other while Tim replied, "Yeh. Right. So long as you and the kid disappear 'n' aren't seen around here no more." Looking back over his shoulder, Tim snarled, "Now cook us up some grub. I'm starvin'."

"We're outta lard," said Agnes sullenly.

"Then borrow some from Missus Fenagen!" Tim ordered. Then to Larry, "And you go back out front 'n' keep watch."

"Right," said Larry, rising and going to the door. "Let me know when the food is ready, all right? I'm starved!" He ducked, turned, and squeezed out the doorway.

Agnes grabbed a shawl and umbrella from the other room.

We were all in a bit of a daze after all that we had heard. Our kohl-eyed commander, however, roused herself.

"Gubby, quick!" said Musetta. "Go with Agnes—keep an eye on her. Maybe you can learn something more."

Tim grabbed Agnes's arm as she passed the table on her way out. "Fenagen's 'n' that's all," he scowled.

By grabbing Agnes, Tim gave Gubbins time to jump onto Agnes's shawl. He climbed to her shoulder as she sullenly left the flat.

When the door shut, Maggot leaned toward Tim in conspiratorial fashion. "We're not really lettin' your sister walk off wi' that kid, are we?"

"Let's just say Big Sis 'n' the brat'll be going to the same place." With that, Tim slowly drew a grimy finger across his own neck, from ear to ear.

Tim's horrific gesture drew another yellow-toothed grin from Maggot. With his low brow tilted forward, Maggot nodded his head in a series of short, spastic nodding fits, coupled with more high-pitched, nasal snickering. "Yeah, same place," he repeated between nods and snickering. "Yeah."

"Awright," said Tim, ending Maggot's weird display. "Where were we?"

"Go fish."

*   *   *

31

A Confusing Concept

"Eeeeeeeeeaaaaaa AAAAAAH—"

"Girls!" shouted Musetta, rousing Ruby and Gracie from their building scream.

"We know the things they're saying are scary," I said, "but we've got to try to think clearly."

"What do we do?" asked the Twins, rallying quickly.

"We've got to split up," said Musetta. "Gubbins is with Agnes. Thursby, why don't you go look for a police officer."

"Right," I agreed. "If the Moon peeks through the clouds, we'll want to be able to tell someone about Bingo."

With a thumb at Tim and Maggot, Musetta continued, "I'll stay here with these charmers and listen for clues. One of us should go 'out front,' wherever that is, with the big fellow called Larry. And one of us should stay with Bingo no matter what happens."

My left upper lip gave a twitch. With Gubbins off with Agnes, that only left four of us. "But . . . that would mean the Twins splitting up."

"I'm sure you'd be all right doing that, wouldn't you girls?"

"Of course!" declared Gracie, letting go of the twin on the right.

"We'd do anything for Bingo!" agreed Ruby with a quick flutter of the wings, which was echoed by Gracie, then Ruby again.

"Good girls!" praised Musetta. "Gracie, why don't you got out front and keep an eye on that Larry fellow?"

"Right!" said Gracie.

"Ruby, you stay with Bingo, all right?"

"Righty-right-right!" said Ruby.

I started toward the table leg nearest the front door. "Gracie," I said, "you come with me and I'll get you set up with Larry before I look for a police officer."

Gracie followed. So did Ruby.

"Ruby," Musetta reminded, pointing at the door to the make-shift nursery, "you need to go the other way, dear. Back in with Bingo, remember?"

"Oh!" said Ruby, clapping her little hands on each side of her face, as did Gracie. They looked at each other with open-mouthed, embarrassed expressions. "I forgot!"

Gracie giggled. Together, they both started running the other way.

"Just Ruby!" I called after Gracie. "You're coming with me, remember? To keep an eye on Larry?"

"Oh my gosh!" said Gracie.

"We're being silly-willies!" said Ruby.

They both, of course, started running toward me.

"Wait, wait, wait," called Musetta. We all joined together again. "Gracie," said Musetta to the twin on the left."

"Yes?"

"Ruby," said Musetta to the twin on the right.

"Yes?"

"Do you know what it means for one of you to be one place and the other to be in a different place?"

"To be *separate*," I added.

Gracie nodded. Ruby shook her head. Each noticed the other's response, then switched: Gracie shook her head, and Ruby nodded.

"Fascinating," I said to Musetta.

"Frustrating," she responded. "Tell you what: You go ahead. Look for the police. I'll work on this."

"Will do," I said. So I ran to the corner of the table and made my way down to the floor. I squeezed under the door and out into the hallway.

More about my own excursion in a moment.

Musetta wisely decided that it was not the time to try to teach the girls the concept of being separated from each other. Instead, she had the Twins remain with Tim and Maggot, with instructions to summon Musetta if either lout got up from the table. Musetta made her way back through the makeshift nursery.

She climbed the radiator and out onto the exterior window sill. The breeze blew harder than before and a misty rain had started. The wind had moved the airship some distance away, so that the rope sloped diagonally up and away from the window sill.

The Flying Fays were still zipping about outside the window, perhaps even more animated than usual. They were spinning circles around the sloping rope, about two-thirds of the way up toward the blimp. Through the rain Musetta spotted the dark figure of the airship at the end of its now-diagonal tether.

"Rumple!" she called out. "RUMPLE!"

The Fays sped up in flying loops around the rope. They flew so fast that they created a figure *O* of light.

The Fays' circle of light caught Musetta's attention again. She looked, first at the circle itself, and then into its center. There was Rumple—walking along the rope like a tightrope walker in a circus. Either he'd gotten lonely, or bored, or perhaps his intuition had told him he was needed.

Whatever the inspiration, our friend was on his way.

*   *   *

32

The Oh-Fudge Factor

In the meantime, I made my way through a dimly lit hallway to a shadowy staircase. The lack of lighting, fortunately, camouflaged the filth. Through the leathery pads of my rabbity feet, I could still feel that gritty, oily veneer that seemed to cover all surfaces.

Two large, musky, shallow-breathing mammals slept in the stairwell. Only as I snuck by them did I realize that they were mammals of the human variety.

The front door had been propped open—perhaps to decrease the oppressive humidity from the storm.

Outside on the tenement building's front steps I spotted the large man named Larry. He stood close against the building with his hands in his jacket pockets and his collar turned up against the wind.

Despite the weather, I didn't have to wait long before I could catch a ride on a passerby. I climbed up to the shoulder of a man wearing wellington boots and a long black slicker. He walked at brisk pace. I figured I would travel up a couple of blocks and back the other direction to see if I could spot a police officer.

Now back to our alleyway acrobat.

When Musetta spotted Rumple toddling along on the tiny, sloping rope, she almost cried out to him. To stop herself, lest she disturb his concentration, she clapped one gloved hand over her mouth in a Twins-like gesture.

In hindsight, though, *concentration* is not the right word. Rumple's tightrope-walking ability, we theorize, had more to do with a *lack* of concentration. Rumple's spontaneous ability as a tightrope walker, in fact, exemplifies an important principle: When we imagine how we *might* fail, we often set ourselves up *to* fail. Rumple, I propose, did not picture all of the possible hazards. He simply did it.

That said, Ladies and Gentlemen, should any of you be presented with an opportunity to tightrope-walk from a moored airship down a steep, slippery, swaying strand hundreds of feet in the air, I suggest that you carefully weigh all risks before undertaking such a venture.

Within seconds after Musetta spotted Rumple, I saw him as well. My wellington-booted gentleman passed the alleyway. Naturally, I looked up toward the window where we had entered. Imagine my shock: High above the alley, barely visible through the rain and against the charcoal-gray storm clouds was the toddling silhouette of a rumplish daredevil.

The stuffiness inside must have inspired Agnes to open up the alley window some more. With the grimy window pulled up, the lamplight allowed me to see Musetta on the exterior window sill.

"Come on, Rumply-wumply," she coaxed. "That's a good Cozy."

After my glimpse of this startling vignette, I popped open my umbrella and descended from the gentleman's shoulder to the street. As I landed, Rumple took that inevitable misstep as the narrow rope swayed with the increasing wind. Rumple pitched forward.

Next exhibit, please.

(Flip-chart Exhibit #9: The "OFDG" Factor.)

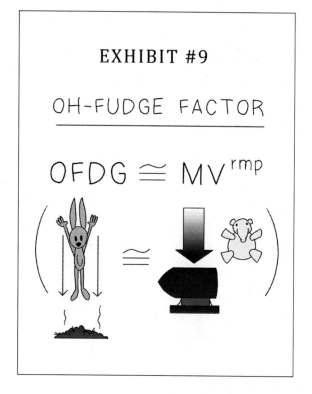

Here we have the mathematical formula that explains, according to the immutable laws of physics, the *O*dds of *F*alling *D*own into the *G*rime, known to mathematicians and scientists as the *O-F-D-G*, or *oh-fudge*, factor. As you see in Exhibit Nine, the OFDG factor is approximately equal to the product of one's mass times one's velocity to the power of *rmp*, or one's rumplishness. The rumplishness of Rumple himself, of course, runs at a fairly constant one hundred percent.

But even the laws of physics are made to be broken—especially for figments of the imagination. Rumple tumbled forward head over feet, from his belly to his head to his back, and so forth. His rubbery consistency combined with the rope's elasticity so that each bounce launched him further through the air. In this manner he covered most of the distance in a mere three bounces.

Alongside each of Rumple's tumbles, the Fays rolled in sympathetic loop-the-loops.

Rumple's last bounce off of the rope propelled him right through the open window. He flew past Musetta so closely that she instinctively ducked.

Rumple careened off the wall and dropped right into the crib.

"Wumpa!" cried Bingo. Child and imaginary friend, together again, hugged each other for all they were worth.

*   *   *

33

Orville and Aggie

While the Twins were being confused at our requests to separate and while Rumple performed his acrobat routine, Gubbins rode along with Agnes. The width of her horizontal head left little room on her shoulder, so Gubbins moved over to her right hand, which clutched the handle of her umbrella. There he stood on the back of Agnes's thumb, holding the umbrella pole like a passenger in a trolley car.

Agnes walked about a block to another tenement building. Before she could turn to go up the front steps into the building, a man stepped out of the shadows. He also held an umbrella, low enough that it obscured his face. He stepped forward quickly, blocking Agnes.

The man raised his umbrella, revealing his face.

"Hello, sweetheart," said the man.

"Orville!"

"I want you to come home, Aggie."

Gubbins immediately liked the man called Orville. Blond curls poked from the edges of his cap. In the tired gaze of his pale blue eyes, Gubbins sensed both kindness and sadness.

"How did ya know I'd be here?" asked Agnes.

"Missus Fenagen said you'd been stoppin' by from time to time. I been out here mosta today, an' parta yesterday and the day before."

"Don't, Orville. It's no use."

"Why? People get past terrible things. They move on wi' their lives!"

"I told ya, I can't. Every time I look at ya, I see his blue eyes, his soft little curls. I smell the smell of him in my arms."

"Ah, Aggie. I love ya . . . an' yer still my wife!"

"It's too late, anyhow. I couldn't come back to ya now if I wanted to."

"What does that mean? What's that no good brother of yours got you mixed up with?"

"Nothing! Stop it!" By now, Agnes's face had contorted tightly, like she was trying to stop up emotions too terrible to let out.

Running around Orville and up the steps, she yelled, "Leave me alone!"

Orville did not follow Agnes up the steps. Before Agnes ducked inside, Gubbins saw Orville lower his head, and his umbrella. He walked off slowly into the darkness and rain.

Inside the building, Agnes collapsed onto stairs past the foyer. Gubbins—who'd moved back onto the small area of Agnes's shoulder—ticked and whirred with confusion. He felt sorry for Agnes, but he didn't know why: She was, after all, a conspirator in the kidnapping of a small child. *Our* small child, our Bingo.

Later, in bits and pieces, we would learn more about Agnes. And by learning more about her, we learned that it is easier to imagine something bad about someone than it is to imagine something good. Probably because it is also easier to imagine something simple than something complex. Imagination, you see, is like a quill pen ready with ink: Anyone can use it to scratch out a simple *X* or an *O*, but it takes hard work and lots of practice to write a poem or draw a picture.

When Agnes had come to our comfy house in the country, something about her worried us. As it turned out, we were right to be concerned. But we let our imaginations scratch out only the easiest of explanations: Agnes was bad, we thought—simple as that.

We didn't try to see the other possibilities. We didn't imagine the rest of the story—that Agnes, although not perfect, was a generally good person. A good person who let herself get caught up in bad situation. A very bad situation.

*   *   *

34

A Bad Pear From the Start

Agnes and her husband, Orville, had married young. People did that more often in those days than in this thoroughly modern era. Agnes and Orville were poor, but usually they were happy. Soon enough, the young couple was blessed with a baby boy.

People who know about such things told the new parents that they could not have any more children. Just the same, Agnes and Orville loved their new baby with their entire souls. That distracted them from disappointment.

We never did learn the name of Agnes and Orville's child, although we suspect, for no particular reason, that they referred to him as their *babkins*.

"Every time I look at ya," we've heard of Agnes telling Orville, "I see his blue eyes, his soft little curls." Such reminders tormented Agnes because her babkins had died from an illness. This happened, sadly, not long after the babe's first birthday.

The parents never recovered from this loss. Parents never do.

Agnes tried to run from her deep and terrible grief by running from Orville. His resemblance to their babkins was too much for Agnes to bear.

Soon afterward, Agnes chanced into a job as a nanny at a beautiful country house north of the Big City. Or south.

As you now know, Agnes had a younger brother named Tim. Much to everyone's misfortune, Tim had been a brutish lout for his entire life.

As a Cozy, of course, it pains me to admit that occasionally there is a child who is rotten from the word go. Humans are like fruit in that regard. Take a pear for example—generally, something must turn a good pear bad. A pear might suffer from neglect, for example, dropping from its tree in perfect condition, only to rot, unnoticed, below. Or a pear might suffer abuse from a heel or a hoof. Ground into a pulp on pasture or prairie, the pear will never have a chance to become a snack, to model for a still-life artist, or to achieve any other goals that a piece of fruit might have.

Once in a while, though, a pear—let's call this pear *Tim*—is shriveled and spotty before he even leaves the tree. If someone nevertheless dares to take a bite, they will discover that Tim is as mushy and bitter and downright disgusting as he looks.

Like Tim the hypothetically horrid pear, Tim the horizontal-headed human was bad from the start.

Despite her little brother's loutishness, Agnes had tried to be a good big sister. Every time he got in trouble and was punished, Tim would promise Agnes that he had learned his lesson. Every time, Agnes would give him the benefit of a doubt.

One might say that she rolled the pear in her hand, time and time again, hoping to find a spot that was not rotten.

Shortly before the events of our story began, Tim was released after a long stretch in prison. As in the past, Agnes wanted to believe that this time was different—that her little brother had finally changed. This hope, and her desperate need to bare her tortured soul to someone, led her to tell her bad-pear brother everything.

"I know I shouldn't of, Your Honorableness," Agnes would later tell a magistrate, as reported in the newspapers. "Only . . . there was no one else to talk to. So I broke down and told that no-good Tim everything. Even about my new job as a nanny at a grand house in the country.

"I was too trusting, I know. What with his past and all. It just didn't seem like anything *could* hurt that family. They were so happy! 'Course, who wouldn't be—all those fine things, and that adorable, healthy little boy."

As guilty people tend to do, Agnes would admit things even while denying them.

"Resent my employers?" she would respond to a question at the inquiry. "Never! They was always kind to me, an' so was Bridie and the others. All sweet. I mean, sometimes it didn't seem fair, that's true enough. That fancy house with hardly any drafts. Always plenty of coal to burn. The way the doctor'd come running at the drop of a hat.

"Sometimes it just didn't seem fair. But I never woulda let anything happen to my baby! I mean, *their* baby. To Bingo."

The inquiring persons at the inquiry would ask: "And after that soul-baring to your newly released brother, the man heretofore referred to as one 'Tim': Did said 'Tim' reveal his nefarious plan to you?"

"Not then, no. Not a hug, not a 'That's too bad'—nothin'. When I was all cried out, Tim was just sittin' there sneering at me, like usual. He did ask about the house—where things was kept and . . . and where the baby slept. My stomach started to turn right then."

The turning of Agnes's stomach, of course, was justified. Tim's time in prison had ripened him into a lout's lout, the loutiest lout of them all. What's more, he had met a fellow jailbird known as Maggot.

The recipe for trouble is simple, Ladies and Gentlemen: Take two louts, add opportunity, and stir well.

As Agnes would later explain: "My brother told me if I didn't help them, he'd do the kidnapping anyway. And if he had to do it without me, they'd hurt the baby. They'd hurt him bad—so they wouldn't have to take care of him while they waited for the money. They said they'd hurt Orville, too—'in case you blab about any of this,' Tim said. I've known Tim his whole life. His eyes told me he meant what he said.

"So I made a deal with the devil, Mister Judge, sir. I just didn't know what else to do. I told him, if he wouldn't hurt the baby, I'd help. Then I'd take the baby away somewhere. Somewhere far, far away, where he couldn't be hurt."

* * *

35

Thick Clouds and Thicker Minds

Now back to our main story. Back to that shadowy, squalid district on that dark and stormy night.

Immediately after watching Rumple's high-flying stunts, I spotted a police officer. Not so much spotted, actually, as *was scooped by*. Fortunately the good officer was walking fairly slowly on his beat. So rather than sending me flying, his shiny right shoe scooped me up and carried me back down the sidewalk in the direction I'd come from.

It turns out that riding a police shoe is fun. Grabbing the front crease of his pant leg for balance, I stood with one well-tractioned rabbity foot forward and one back. The most comparable human activity might be standing on the foredeck of a small sloop. Picture such a boat rocking forward and back while crashing over the waves of a choppy sea.

Not that I've ever had such a boat ride. But I imagine it's something like riding on a police officer's shoe.

My outing had proved successful: Specifically, it proved that the police did patrol past the kidnappers' hideout. Good to know, but for the time being I had no way of communicating with humans. The thick clouds above removed any chance that a thin stream of moonlight might work its way through.

So my good officer knew nothing of the nattily dressed individual who rode on the well-polished shoe of his right foot. Nor could he detect a certain jumble of mechanical bits standing on the umbrella-holding hand of a certain sullen, horizontal-headed woman approaching from the other direction.

Gubbins and I saw each other, though. Holding Agnes's umbrella shaft with one hand, my chum waved at me with the other and called "Tr-r-r-r-r-r-r-!"

My police officer passed by the front stairs of the hideout tenement. Agnes neared. On seeing the officer, she immediately lowered the rim of her umbrella to avoid making eye contact. She quickened her pace.

My vigilant officer would have none of it.

"Evening, ma'am," he said loudly, stopping in front of Agnes. "Everything all right? Not safe for a woman to be out by herself around here."

"We were outta *lard!*" Agnes declared. She twisted her side toward the officer to draw attention to the tin, presumably filled with lard, tucked under her left arm. Then she veered off toward the stairs.

I dismounted from the officer's shoe and grabbed a handful of skirt pleat as Agnes passed. I started climbing the side of her skirt so I could accompany her and Gubbins inside.

A guilty mind, no doubt, prevented Agnes from acting naturally. As she started up the stairs, she couldn't help raising her umbrella to look at Larry. He still lurked at the top of the stairs in his role as lookout.

Larry attempted to shrink further into the shadows, but his bulky form didn't allow for much shrinking. His own guilty expression was left protruding into the light from the open entry door.

Thank goodness for the thick-headedness of the criminal mind. Rather than ignoring Agnes and calmly engaging the police officer in conversation, Larry continued to stare, wide-eyed and open-mouthed, at the officer. But for the lack of prison stripes, he looked like an escaping convict caught in a spotlight. He lumbered inside after Agnes, pulling the entry door shut behind him.

"What'd that copper want?" Larry asked Agnes while continuing to watch the police officer watch them.

"How should I know? If he knew anything, he wouldn't just be standing there."

"'S'pose not. I don't like this, though. I'm startin' not to like any a' this—includin' what Dave said about the kid."

"You think I like it any better? But I will *not* let them hurt that baby. As God is my witness!" Agnes turned to go up the dimly lit stairs.

In a louder voice, Larry said, "How you gonna stop 'em?"

Agnes slowed for a moment, but she neither stopped climbing the stairs nor replied.

Our police officer went on his way, down the shadowy sidewalk through the rain. He did not yet have enough information to act. As an astute *policier*, though, he had taken note of all he'd observed. This brief interaction would prove most important later, after the next great adventures of that desperate night.

*   *   *

36

A Desperate Decision

Upstairs in the hideout, we found the Twins still keeping watch on the card table. Well, sort of keeping watch.

"No fair!" we heard one twin protest as we climbed the table leg. "You skipped Harriet! Now you have to go back to Buster and start over."

"Do not!" countered the first twin's counterpart. "If you do a pirouette on Simon, you get to skip Harriet."

Gubbins and I peeked over the table edge. Just then Ruby launched into a standing broad jump off of a tobacco-juice stain toward a schmear of roach remains.

"Oof!" Ruby grunted on landing. "Made it! I'm all the way to Georgina this time!"

"That's George, not Georgina," said Gracie.

"No, see the way her antennas have dried? It's like a little bow."

"Anyway, you're making up rules," Gracie complained. Her wings fluttered as she balanced on one leg on half a flattened roach. From there she hopped diagonally to what appeared to be the late roach's other half.

Ruby paused, thinking, then giggled. "We made up *all* the rules!" she laughed.

Gracie giggled. "Anytime anyone makes up more rules, the rule is they have to go touch Sneery McUgly's shirt sleeve."

Ruby let out a short, delighted scream that ended as laughter: "Aaaaaahah-hah-hah! Gross! They do not!"

"Do so. Starting . . . now!"

By this time, Gubbins and I were practically standing in front of the Twins. "Hello, girls," I said.

"Thursby!" cried Gracie

"Gubbins!" cried Ruby.

"I say, you didn't happen to notice Agnes pass through?" I was teasing my little friends. Agnes had gone right past them to the makeshift nursery when we entered. Larry, by the way, had stayed out front after the officer went on his way.

"Agnes?" asked Gracie. "I thought we were supposed to watch Tim and Dave!"

"Sneery McUgly and Maggot," Ruby clarified.

"True enough," I acknowledged. "So did anything happen with, um, Sneery McUgly and Maggot?"

"Not much," said Gracie. "They almost had a knife fight."

"A knife fight," I said to Gubbins. "We should be so lucky."

"It was boring," said Ruby with a scrunched up face. "So we made up a game!"

Agnes swept back into front room with Musetta clinging to dress pleats on the near side. Musetta jumped from dress to table as Agnes passed to the kitchen corner of the room.

Agnes said to the louts, "The baby's in there jabbering away to himself!"

"Maybe that'll keep the brat from screamin' for five minutes," mumbled Sneery McUgly . . . Tim, rather.

"Yeah," muttered Maggot, "keep da brat from screamin'."

Since I'd seen Musetta last, hope had joined the intensity in her eyes. The hope that comes with a plan.

"I was watching the Fays flying above the alley," she said. "They swirled in the air, then let themselves drift on the wind. Every time it carried them back in the direction we came from—fast!"

"To the north?" I asked.

"Yes!" she confirmed. "Or south!"

Gubbins whirred with excitement.

We had all realized that the situation was not likely to change before morning. We needed help . . . human help.

There were only two questions: First, to whom should we go for help? Second, how would we communicate with them? Third—

Three questions. There were *three* questions: to whom, how, and . . . could we make it there and back in time?

★   ★   ★

37

No Time to Gawk

We left Rumple happily ensconced in the crib with Bingo, and the Twins playing their morbid hopscotch game on the table.

Still tethered to the outside sill, the *Starry Night* tilted and careened like a kite, as if it might overturn on any pass and crash to Earth.

I looped my legs and bent one arm over the tugboat-winch rope so that I was hanging beneath it. Then I popped open my umbrella and found myself shooting along the wet, diagonal thread, the umbrella working like a wind-filled sail to drag me upward. Closer to the airship, the rope's angle grew more steep. I pulled myself hand-over-hand up the last few yards. Fortunately I was facing up—so I need not look down—as I swayed back and forth in the rain and wind.

Once aboard, I used the winch to bring Musetta and Gubbins aboard.

We waved at the Fays, but they would not follow. We left them floating outside the makeshift nursery in the airspace of the alley.

Our flight home was a mad dash compared to our leisurely journey before. The *Starry Night* covered the same distance in a quarter of the time with the powerful wind at our back. We hardly needed the propeller at all, although Gubbins worked the rudders and elevators constantly to keep the blimp on course.

The low, thick cover of dark clouds, we discovered, extended all the way back to the grand house and beyond. Along the way, though, the three of us developed a plan—a plan we christened *Operation Moonlight*.

"We're all agreed then?" I half-shouted so that Gubbins could hear as well.

"Whir-tik-whir-whirrrrr!" replied Gubbins from the velocipede engine.

"Agreed!" called Musetta as she stood up from her seat on the stack of supplies. She opened a large sea chest much like the one at the foot of Great-grandfather's bed, except much smaller, of course. Who knows? As a lad, little Augie might have created our sea chest when he first dreamed of seafaring adventure.

Out of the sea chest Musetta pulled a stout cutlass in a black scabbard. From the base of the sword's grip, a fanciful brass hilt-guard fanned out and wrapped forward in the form of a fish's tail. Musetta draped the scabbard's broad belt over one shoulder like a bandolier. The weapon hung ready at her side.

"I've always wanted to wear one of these!" she crowed.

Moments later, we almost missed our destination. No lights were turned up in the house, leaving the estate camouflaged by the shadowy landscape. Only a brief release of atmospheric electricity—that is to say, lightning—revealed the location.

"We're right over it!" Musetta and I yelled together, even as Gubbins shifted the airship into a steep turn.

With the propeller's force balanced against the wind, we held steady above the chimney. Gubbins then lowered the airship straight down using the elevators. His piloting skills had improved so quickly that I was able to step from our gondola right onto the chimney top.

"Best of luck, mates!" I shouted as Gubbins directed the airship up and away from the rooftop.

"Right back at ya, bunny-boy!" called Musetta with a broad salute. She stood at the front end of the gondola, holding on to one of the cables attaching gondola to blimp. Leaning out over the dash of the elephant saddle, fishtail cutlass at her side, Musetta was at once beautiful and utterly dashing.

But there was no time to gawk. I popped open my trusty umbrella and leapt into the chimney's blackness.

(The speaker receives a signal from his assistant.)

Hm? The time? Oh, yes! So sorry, Ladies and Gentlemen. A figment eats only when a treat sounds tasty. We lack the lunch-hour reminder of a rumbling tummy.

Let us break now for lunch. When we return, we'll learn what an old pirate-fighter can do when faced with a nest of louts.

(lunch break)

PART FIVE

The Old Pirate Fighter

38

Approaching Opa

No, it's no use slouching down—we see you back there! I hope it won't be necessary to summon the constabulary!

(There follows an unfortunate disruption in the proceedings. Several Absinthe conference goers create a diversion in the back of the Jungfrau Room. One of their confederates throws his hat over the guest speaker and attempts to abduct him. A chase ensues, wreaking havoc in the lecture hall. With the assistance of audience members, the mêlée is eventually brought to a safe conclusion. The offending parties are escorted bodily from the building.

The conference organizers come onto the stage and offer their humble apologies to the audience and the guest speaker for the disruption.

The speaker is placed back on the central table onstage. He returns to his podium. He takes a moment to smooth his ruffled ears and straighten his waistcoat.)

Really, no apologies are necessary—I'm fine. Thank you.

Let us not dwell on incursions from the Matterhorn Room. After all, we have our own adventure story to continue. And what an adventure we still faced on that tempestuous night!

Now. Where did we leave off at the break? Ah, yes.

The chimney's interior was cool. No one had made a fire, despite the bad weather. Such luxuries were forgotten in that time of distress.

As I mentioned, the house was utterly dark. Father had left for the Big City to try to find a banker who would permit a late-night cash withdrawal for the ransom money. Father had agreed to pay the kidnappers in order to try to get Bingo home safely.

Mother was in bed, still sick with fear and grief; Bridie slept in a chair beside the bed. Michael and Abigail the cook were out with search parties. They were unaware of the telephone call from the kidnappers. Father hadn't told anyone, for fear that the louts would harm Bingo.

So our question of *To whom?* had been answered for us: We would turn to Great-grandfather for help. Great-grandfather had been my choice for assistance, in any case. Rare is the adult who will listen calmly to a figment of the imagination and act on said figment's say-so. I hoped that my past association with Great-grandfather would give us at least a chance of a favorable response.

The *How?* was now the trick.

Poor Dandie—distraught by Bingo's disappearance, no doubt, and either blessed or cursed by a lack of further understanding—waited faithfully, staring at the front door. Sensing my arrival, he charged into the drawing room to the hearth.

I leapt out of the fireplace and straddled Dandie's neck. "Go get Opa!" I urged firmly but gently, having learned from Musetta. "Go get Opa!"

The Dinmont's intuition impressed me once again. Or maybe he felt guilty for declining to act as our caravan to the Big City. In any event, we were off and running. Like Paul Revere's steed, Dandie flew fearless and fleet. He dashed to the foyer, galloped up the stairs, and sprinted down the hallway.

Great-grandfather's bedroom door stood open. Bridie had probably left it open to reduce the steamy pressure of a stormy night. The hound understood exactly—he rounded the corner right into the bedroom.

Great-grandfather slept in the same four-poster bed in which he'd been born.

Dandie pounced up against the bedside, setting his forepaws up as far as he could. I climbed over his fur tuft and snout to the bed. From there I climbed onto the old boy's chest.

I watched for signs of dreaming. They were all there—flickering eyelids, twitching lips, fidgeting limbs. Great-grandfather was active in the world of dreams. No one is old there!

"Augie!" I whispered, hoping to sow the seeds of communication. "It's Thursby, your friend from long ago!"

In his sleep, Great-grandfather's twitching lips formed my name with only a breath of sound behind it, "Thursby."

"Do you remember me?" I pressed. "Smallish chap in a natty green jacket? Head of a lop-eared rabbit?"

"Huh?" grunted Great-grandfather, opening his eyes into a little squint. He blinked several times, then asked, "Someone there?" He glanced to his left at the windows, which strained against the storm outside.

Dandie gave a soft "Wuf!" to say hello to the man whom he knew, like Bingo, as *Opa*.

Great-grandfather looked to his right at Dandie's snout, peeking over the bed's edge.

With considerable effort, Great-grandfather scooted closer to Dandie. He reached over with his right hand—that being his stronger side—to scratch the dog's fluffy head and behind his ears. "That big ol' storm scaring you? Hm?"

Still the sweet, caring boy I remembered—doing his best to calm a little dog during a thunder storm.

A brief crackling of light filled the room with a series of pulsing illuminations. The sudden light cast an immense and frightening shadow on the wall behind Dandie—a hulking shadow shaped like the silhouette of large man wearing a cutaway coat. A beast of a man with thick, wild locks of hair in unacceptable disarray. The silhouette, one might think, of a pirate!

Of course, the beastly man was me, still standing on Great-grandfather's chest, and still only half a foot tall with ears lifted. I hadn't realized it, but the *Dinmont ride of Thursby Revere* had left my velveteen gonfalons outrageously askew. I immediately set things straight, or rather, rearranged the floppiness.

It was too late.

Still half asleep—when humans see things they otherwise wouldn't—Great-grandfather had witnessed the primitive projection on the wall. Now, though, his eyelids had popped open wide. Well, his right eye, anyway, but he was definitely awake.

The old pirate-fighter pulled his hand away from Dandie. Slowly and slyly, he reached over beside his headboard.

"Who's there?!" he challenged, swinging his walking stick at the imagined, wild-haired intruder, and on across the bed. I dove to one side to avoid his arm. "Who's there I say?!"

Another series of bright flashes came from outside. The lightning revealed nothing more than Dandie, rounding the corner into the hallway at a dead run. The dog peered cautiously back around the doorjamb.

"I'm sorry, Augie," I said, unheard. "I am so sorry."

Great-grandfather lowered his walking stick onto the bed and let his head drop back to the pillow. That short bit of exertion, and the fright, had exhausted him.

"Losing my mind," he whispered to himself in gasps. "Losing my *mind*."

*   *   *

3 9

Operation Moonlight

While I was busy inside, Gubbins and Musetta put Operation Moonlight into effect.

Gubbins allowed the wind to push the *Starry Night* along. At the same time, he worked the rudders and elevators to move the airship. The goal was that spot in the clouds directly between the grand house and the Moon.

Up, up, and further up!

Though not so far up as before. They didn't need to fly as high as Rumple had gone. Or even as high as our flight over the countryside's pasture-work quilt.

The storm clouds drooped low, you see, like an awning heavy with rainwater. But with the sky so dark, and with the rain falling in dense sheets, Musetta and Gubbins had no idea how close those clouds were.

Until, that is, *WHOOMPF!* The *Starry Night* bounced against the clouds' sopping, spongy, spilling underbelly. The bounce vibrated through the cloud shelf—the same vibration that usually occurs when two storm clouds collide, resulting in what we call *rolling thunder.*

As the thunder rolled, the airship rattled—as did its occupants.

"WHAT WAS *THAT*?!" Musetta shouted from her position at the front of the elephant saddle. She realized that Gubbins couldn't have heard her. She could hardly hear herself!

An electric flash snapped through the soaked atmosphere, exposing the scene: They had reached their target. The top of the blimp's front end continued to bump against the underside of the roiling cloud shelf like a calf nuzzling its mother. Rain from the charcoal-gray ceiling poured over and around them.

Musetta climbed to the back of the gondola. Gubbins was still pedaling for all he was worth. He was not trying to move forward, you understand, but simply to steady the airship against the wind and rain.

"WE'RE THERE!" Musetta shouted over the wind and rain and thunder. Pointing overhead, she added, "I'M GOING UP!"

Gubbins could only nod quickly. Keeping the airship from spinning out of control took all his concentration.

Musetta waited for the next, inevitable white flash. When the electric pulses revealed the scene, she gauged how and where to begin her climb.

Imagine, Ladies and Gentlemen! As high in the sky as the clouds themselves, in the middle of a terrible thunder storm, battered by the elements! With only flickering, ghostly images to go by, Musetta grabbed ahold of suspension cables on the blimp's underside. Her feet hanging, she climbed, hand over hand.

Once up the side far enough, she pressed her toes against the airship and used the horizontal cables, where possible, as footholds as well as handholds. All the while, the wind and rain crashed against her. And let me tell you, my friends, a single raindrop is to a Cozy what a bucket of water might be to a human. Well, a large glassful, anyway.

Musetta reached the airship's rounded top. She pushed locks of her drenched hair back from her eyes and straightened her tiara. She drew the fishtail cutlass from its scabbard and waited for the next flash of lightning.

An electric explosion lit up the sky. The cloud shelf was right above her head. Musetta slashed upward, striking a gash in the roiling nebulousness. A torrent of water spilled from the opened storm cloud like a waterfall. The rush of water slammed Musetta against the airship's top and washed her down along its slope. At the same time the water's weight forced the *Starry Night* into a downward spiral.

Spinning downward in the darkness and water, Musetta groped for something to grab. Just as the momentum of the spin swung her feet over the blimp's curve, she caught a suspension cable with her free hand.

Working the rudders and elevators frantically, pedaling furiously, Gubbins pulled the vessel out of its spiral and leveled it off. They pulled away from the torrent of rainwater.

Musetta climbed back to the blimp's top. She drew one gloved forearm across her kohled eyes and looked up. The slashed opening in the cloud had split open further with the force of the water. But no moonlight.

"IT'S NOT ENOUGH!" she hollered over the side at the back of the blimp. "FURTHER ALONG! FURTHER ALONG!"

She waited a second, then felt the airship rising again toward the storm clouds. Gubbins had heard her!

Again the *Starry Night* fought through the storm's fury. This time, instead of holding the nose of the airship against the cloud shelf, Gubbins guided the vessel along right below it.

Although Musetta knew Gubbins couldn't hear her, she couldn't help raving, "Excellent, Gubby! You read my mind!"

For extra stability, Musetta knelt down on the blimp's top, near the nose. She gripped the cutlass hilt tightly with both hands behind the fanciful fishtail hilt.

With the next flash of lightning, she slashed again into the gray sponge above. Again the rainwater stored up in the soaked cloud flooded down upon her.

This time Gubbins was ready. When the water hit, he held the airship on a steady course.

Instead of slashing through, Musetta held the cutlass straight up. As the airship moved slowly forward, the cutlass split a longer and longer gash in the underside of the cloud.

The icy rainwater crashed down upon Musetta as if she was bathing under Niagara Falls. She held firm.

The water spilled over the blimp and over Gubbins as well. He pedaled onward, driving the airship along beneath the storm-cloud Niagara.

The sky was illuminated yet again, and in the first instant, Gubbins thought it was simply more lightning. But it did not flicker and go away. When he felt the caress of a pale glow on his shoulder, he knew: Moonlight!

Gubbins turned and looked behind them. The long opening, carved by Musetta's cutlass, was peeling apart under the tension of the cloud's weight and the force of escaping water. The obscuring nebulosity was splitting in two.

Instead of rain, *moonlight* spilled through.

Gubbins piloted the *Starry Night* down, away from the clouds. As they left the rainwater cascade, Musetta too saw the opening they had wrought. The Moon—more piercingly bright than either had ever seen—smiled broadly at the two battle-fatigued Cozies. It was as if the celestial orb had expected them at that very moment.

★   ★   ★

40

The Call to Glory

Back on terra firma, I could only await the results of Operation Moonlight. From one corner of the bed, I watched out the window and into the darkness.

The wild-haired shadow intruder had knocked Great-grandfather for a loop, as they say nowadays. But the old pirate-fighter soon rallied.

"Steady, you old coot," he whispered to himself. "After the masts fell, only a matter of time before the demons started boarding." He looked at the bedroom windows. "Fresh air—that's what I need."

Standing was a slow and excruciating process—for Great-grandfather to do and for me to watch. He shuffled a few steps, then let himself drop into his wheelchair. He grabbed his knitted blanket from on top of the sea chest at the foot of his bed and draped it over his lap. Then he wheeled himself over to the bedroom window. With his walking stick, he deftly unlocked the latch and opened the window.

A cool and blustery gale washed over him, filling the room with the storm's scent.

Great-grandfather sat with his eyes closed and his face angled up, enjoying the fresh, stormy air.

"Ahhhhh. Takes me back," he said. He inhaled deeply and exhaled with a satisfied sigh, "Like being at sea again. Clears the mind."

At the same time, the open window afforded me a better view. Out through the darkness, a steady light appeared in the sky. Light that did not flicker or flash.

Dare I hope?

The small line of light broadened, grew brighter. The edges of a parting in the cloud cover became visible. The opening expanded, revealing a steady, piercing brightness.

Operation Moonlight had succeeded!

The bright round face of the Moon peeked through. A pale, rectangular illumination stretched across the room.

As if the moonlight were a celestial finger pointing at something, Great-grandfather cocked his head to one side. Slowly, looking over his shoulder, he used his good arm to wheel his chair in a clockwise circle.

He fixed his gaze on me. A gleam of recognition came into his eyes.

"*You,*" he gasped, "—from the nursery!"

"Hello, Augie," I said.

"You . . . can't . . . be real."

"No, my boy, I'm not 'real'—not as you mean. But your mind has not failed you—I am *here*. Point of fact, I've been here all these many years."

"I'm out of my senses."

"No, Augie. It's time for you to *come* to your senses—time to help your great-grandson!"

"What's that?" he grunted. "My grandson? What are you talking about?!"

"He's been kidnapped, old bean."

"Kidnapped?!"

"By a dastardly lot."

"No!" he said, tears welling in his eyes. "When?!"

"Yesterday in the early morning hours. Now the kidnappers have him in the Big City, and I know where. I've come to lead you to them."

He shook his head. "There's nothing *I* can do." He clenched his eyes tightly shut. "Not any more. Look at me!"

"*Stop it*, boy. There is no time to waste! You are Bingo's only hope. Now stop thinking about what you can't do, and try picturing what you *can*!"

Great-grandfather opened his eyes again. He turned himself to look out at the storm.

I leapt from bed to sea chest and, using my umbrella, down to the floor. Then I ran over and climbed up to the old fellow's knee.

He was squinting at the sliver of the Moon still visible in the distance. Already the clouds were pulling together again, closing off the moonlight. Nevertheless, that silvery sliver sparkled in Great-grandfather's eyes like the flashing light of ideas in his mind.

"Maybe if . . . Bridie . . . then Nellie . . . that shortcut past old MacDonald's place . . ."

He wheeled back to the foot of the bed, beside the travel-worn sea chest. He opened the lid. I couldn't help thinking that if I'd gotten into *that* trunk all those years ago, I might've really gone to sea!

From deep inside the chest, Great-grandfather pulled a stack of folded clothing. The clothes looked black in the faint light. When he shook the piece on top to unfold it, I recognized it at once: a blue woolen frock with white piping on the collar and cuffs.

His uniform from the Navy.

"If we're going into battle," he said, "I'd better dress the part."

* * *

41

Rekindling the Flame

Great-grandfather's uniform hung loosely on his agéd frame, but it inflated his spirit like a puffed up rooster. To the extent that a partially paralyzed septuagenarian can puff up, that is—and I tell you he can! Not only in the way he held his head up so straight. It was in his eyes: The flame of a pirate-fighter's soul burned there again.

He was—at least for that night—*Augie* again.

While dressing, Augie had used his imagination to formulate a plan for getting us to the Big City post haste. He set about implementing that plan without further delay.

Some of you might think that I am stretching a bit to insert our theme of *imagination* at this juncture. You might say that deciding what needs to be done and doing it is not imagination, it's simply planning. If so, then perhaps I have been too subtle regarding Gubbins' and Musetta's imaginative ideas that helped us find little Bingo in the first place.

Let me be clear: There is far more to *imagination* than conjuring up figments like lop-eared-rabbit-headed gentleman Cozies. Not more important, obviously, but still. Imagination is the key to all good, Ladies and Gentlemen, whether used to build a bridge or to sympathize with others. It is the ability to picture what does not yet exist, and to feel what has never been felt.

For example, those of us still in our prime will need to use our imaginations to picture what that night must have been like for Augie—a human not only of advanced age, but a survivor of apoplexy as well. By the time he had donned his uniform, Augie dropped back into his wheelchair, breathing heavily. We hadn't even left yet, and his body felt the strain.

"The uniform looks great, Augie," I said, making my way up to his shoulder. He needed a second to catch his breath.

"Feels good, too," he replied. Then he glanced over at me on his shoulder. "Thursby, are you sure I'm not going mad?"

"You are *not* going mad—"

"—said the rabbit-headed fellow standing on my shoulder."

"Point taken. But figments born in the imaginations of the insane are neither helpful, nor attractive, nor good dressers. And, well . . ." I gave a short wave of one hand to gesture at myself. Not out of vanity, of course. As I'm sure you will agree, it's quite obvious that I do not hail from the *Albtraumwelt.*

"Hm," Augie said, not particularly reassured. "I'll take your word for it."

Suddenly, from the doorway: *"Athair Críonna!"*

*   *   *

42

Caught!

There stood Bridie, holding up a lantern and staring right at us. I looked at Augie, he looked at me, we both looked at Bridie. Would she faint on seeing a nursery figment standing on Athair Críonna's shoulder?

"What're you doin' with your window open on a night like this?" Bridie exclaimed. She entered and she walked right past Augie—and me—to shut and latch the window. "You'll catch your death!"

She had not seen me!

Only then did I notice: The moonlight was gone. Out the window, once again only subtle charcoal shades were visible in the general darkness. With the movement of the clouds and the arc of the Moon through the sky, we had known our opportunity would be short-lived.

I waved at Augie. He looked right at me on his shoulder.

"What is it?" he whispered.

"Just checking," I said.

As you would expect, without moonlight Bridie could not see me. But now that he had spotted me, Augie *continued* to see me! This astonished and pleased me, since we still had much to do. It also concerned me, as I shall explain in a bit.

Bridie turned away from the window and squinted at Augie.

"What a wild look in your eyes," she remarked. "Did the storm frighten you, you ol' dear?"

I leaned in close to Augie's ear. "Go on," I urged.

Bridie held her lantern closer, noticing Augie's uniform. "Now what's that costume you're wearing?"

"Go *on*, boy," I urged again.

"Bridie," said Augie, "I've had a dream."

Her mouth dropped open. "*Begorrah,*" she gasped. Augie knew that, on hearing certain words—like *dream, vision,* or *premonition*—Bridie was ready to be amazed.

Augie went on, "A strange being appeared to me—"

"A strange *and magical* being," I suggested.

"A strange and—" Augie looked askance at me on his shoulder, then continued, "—magical being. A tiny fellow with the head of a rabbit."

"*M'anam!*"

"An English lop rabbit," I offered. In the excitement, Augie failed to add these details.

Instead he cut to the chase, announcing, "He told me where Bingo is being held."

Bridie stumbled backward. "Athair Críonna! I didna' know anyone'd told ya the boy'd been taken!"

"No one had, Bridie. Not until my dream."

"A messenger! A messenger from the land o' the fairies! Oh my heavens. Oh my stars! There's no one to go to, nothin' to do! The telephone is down for the storm, and everyone else is away! And I couldn't leave the missus, not in her state!"

"Drat!" exclaimed Augie with a sidelong glance in my direction. "The telephone is down!" Truth be told, the family's recently installed telephone had not occurred to either of us. This was embarrassing for me, in particular, since the louts had mentioned telephoning Father earlier. But Augie and I were children of another era.

Anyway, the storm had rendered the new telephone a moot point. So we went with our original idea: to go to the Big City ourselves.

In the interest of time, I will move quickly through the actual preparation for my and Augie's departure. Simply put, we could not have done it without Bridie. She helped to get Athair Críonna down the stairs. She harnessed Nellie to the tilbury carriage. Finally, she boosted Augie up onto the carriage's bench seat.

Poor Bridie's rosy cheeks turned practically purple from the exertion.

"Oh, me," she said to herself as we charged away into the night. "What've I done?"

★   ★   ★

43

A Wild Ride in a Tilbury Carriage

Through his Sunday jaunts of old, Augie knew the back roads well. The shortcut to the Big City, though, offered no graded and maintained highway. In those days, even the main country roads were simply dirt tracks. Back roads were hardly more than mud-filled ruts between slippery rises and falls.

But nothing slowed us. Nellie must have sensed the urgency. Without more than a tap on her haunches ever, she raced through the squally night.

The water and mud spinning off of the carriage's two large, white-washed wheels pelted us as mercilessly as the rain.

Augie leaned to the left in the carriage to pin down his bad side while controlling the reins with his good. His teeth were clenched and his lips tight. An almost frenzied intensity had overtaken his eyes, as if he fast approached a ship flying the Jolly Roger.

I sat beside Augie on the bench seat—bounced on the seat, more like. I would bounce, bounce, bounce further and further from Augie's side until I was nearly bounced out of the carriage. Then I'd bounce, bounce, bounce back again. Why, one might think I was a figment based on some uncouth, ill-mannered jack rabbit rather than an English lop of top-tier deportment!

When I was lucky, I'd land in a seated position. When less lucky, in some more ignoble pose.

"Almost had a man overboard there!" shouted Augie after a bad bump had nearly jolted us both onto the road. I do mean *very* nearly. The jolt had left me hanging from the dash rail in one of those less-than-dignified positions.

I held on tight until Augie had a chance to reach forward and set me back on the seat. "You'd a' made a good sailor, Thursby, old friend!" he proclaimed.

That remark has meant much to me over the years since.

As we closed on the Big City, the roads improved. The night waned, and with it, the storm. Having paid close attention to the main thoroughfares from our bird's eye view on the *Starry Night*, I was able to direct Augie to the louts' hideout.

My sense of direction faltered only once or twice, requiring a brief retracing of Nellie's steps. Those occasions inspired Augie to relive his days at sea in the form of salty language. Decorum demands the omission of such language here. I *can* say that the originator of such expressions must have had an impressive imagination, particularly with regard to anatomical rearrangements.

Only hours had passed, but dawn's pale glow made the neighborhood of the hideout feel like a place I'd known long before. Different, but vaguely familiar. While the coming light decreased the eeriness somewhat, it exposed the squalor all the more.

I'd hoped our timing would put us in front of the tenement entrance as the officer passed by on patrol. No such luck. The street was deserted.

Deserted, that is, until the Flying Fays *swooshed* in front of us, then back and forth and around us. Swoosh! Swoosh-swoosh! Swoosh!

"What in the Sam Hill?!" said Augie. Apparently his figment-awareness also made the light-sprites visible to him.

"Friends of mine," I explained.

"Might've guessed."

Having checked on our arrival, the Fays zipped back to their spot outside the alley window.

My concern for Augie was only increasing. Even though the Moon was long gone and daylight was filling the sky, he had spotted the Fays and continued to see me. First things first, I thought—and that means Bingo.

Augie struggled out of the tilbury with me again on his shoulder. Once on the pavement, the old fellow gazed around somewhat dazed, like a sailor trying to get his land-legs back after a long time at sea.

"It'll be all right, Augie," I said.

"Of course. Bingo—he's all that matters now." Augie frowned with determination and started forward.

Only as Augie lurched up the outside stairs did a still figure beside the entry doors catch my attention—Larry, the louts' lookout.

*   *   *

44

One Less Loutish Lout
and a Sullen Ex-Nanny

Eyes as wide open as his mouth, Larry, the largest and some-what less loutish lout, stared at the approaching Augie in much the same way that he'd stared at the police officer.

There's no denying that Augie must have appeared somewhat deranged, what with his loose-fitting, antique naval uniform, his wisps of remnant hair, his lurching gate, and his one arm flopping about.

Not that I wasn't a sight to behold myself, mind you, but I enjoyed the benefit of being invisible to most. More than a few of you, I would guess, have wished you were invisible at times, hm? Perhaps after a spot of lunch has dribbled its way onto your shirt or blouse?

(A number of audience members check their own shirts and blouses for stains.)

Riding on Augie's shoulder while he made his way up the front steps reminded me of my ride on the police officer's shoe the prior evening. More rodeo-like, though, I imagine, as the old fellow would heave himself up with his good leg, followed by a swaying to catch his balance. The swaying provided momentum that he would then throw into another heave to step upward, followed by another swaying, and so forth. This provided a far more fitful ride than the peace officer's steady stride.

"Ignore the big one there," I counseled. "I don't think he's a threat."

It wasn't until we were entering the building that Larry tried, clumsily, to intervene. "Hey!" he said as we passed him and went inside. "Hey!"

"Upstairs," I said to Augie. "Third floor."

"Hey! Where are you going?" Larry followed us up the stairs, right behind Augie but limiting himself to similar inanities: "Hey, I'm talkin' to you. Do you live here or somethin'? Where you goin'? Hey!" *Et cetera.*

The trip up to the third floor was hard on Augie. Yet I think he would've bowled over anyone in his path.

Between the second and third floors, we passed the sleeping mammals without rousing them from hibernation. This was good, if only because movement might have further distributed their *au naturale* scent.

As we neared the third floor, Larry dared to reach out and tug on the back of Augie's uniform. "Now look, mister—" Larry started.

Still gripping the stairway rail with his right hand, Augie spun his shoulders and turned his head quickly to the left. His bad arm flailed out, more like a potential weapon than dead weight. His pirate-fighter's eyes shot a gaze like daggers down at Larry with enough vehemence to pierce the softish lout's big frame. Larry immediately stepped down several steps on the staircase. He seemed to deflate before our eyes.

Augie's perspiring, flushed, and wildly wispy-haired head trembled. He held his gaze on Larry. The big man continued a slow, backward retreat down the steps. "All right, all right, mister. Take it easy. You can't just . . . There's no reason . . . I . . . I . . . ."

With that, Larry, the lout who seemed less loutish, who was at least three times Augie's size, turned and ran down the stairs.

We finally reached the third floor. Augie paused for only a few seconds to catch his breath.

"Which one," he puffed.

"Straight ahead." I pointed at the door in front of us. "It might be unlocked."

Augie stepped to the door and turned the knob—sure enough: unlocked. He swung the door open.

"Aaaaaaa!" screamed Agnes at the sight of the wild-eyed intruder. Then she recognized him as Athair Críonna. "Sir!"

"The jig is up, Agnes!" announced Augie, entering by lurches. "Where is the boy?"

Agnes hung her horizontal head forward. "This way, Sir," she said sullenly. "He's all right, I promise. I never would've let any harm come to him."

We followed Agnes into the makeshift nursery. Bingo was standing in his crib, listening. Rumple stood beside him.

"Opa!" cried Bingo on seeing his great-grandfather enter the room. Holding his arms out, Bingo launched into a wailing fit of exhaustion and relief. Great-grandfather scooped great-grandson into his one good arm.

Bingo half-turned back toward the crib. "Bumpa," he said through his tears.

Augie leaned Bingo over the crib so he could grab what Augie thought was a toy until Rumple jumped up to meet Bingo's outstretched arms.

Staring at the strange little creature in his grandson's arms, Augie opened the right side of his mouth to request an explanation, when Agnes asked—

"Did they catch them when they went to get the money?"

"If you're talking about the oafish conspirator who was supposed to be keeping watch, he ran away like a coward."

"What about my brother, and Maggot?"

"Er, Augie," I said, "perhaps I should have mentioned . . ."

He gave me an arch look. "There are others?"

Note to self, I thought: Prior to confronting a gang of kidnappers, discuss number of such.

Agnes's expression went from sullen to fearful. "You mean they're still out there?"

Right behind us, from the entrance to the makeshift nursery, came a voice—a low, brutish voice: "Well, well, well. Looks like the Marines have landed."

⋆   ⋆   ⋆

45

<h1 style="text-align:center">First Mate Augustus versus The Louts, Part 1</h1>

"Hurrah!" came a tiny, happy voice immediately after the brutish one from the doorway.

"Hurrah for Bingo's great-grandpa!" shouted Ruby merrily. The Twins were perched on the brim of Tim's bowler hat, their feet dangling off the front.

"Thursby, look!" called Gracie. "We're riding on Sneery McUgly's hat!"

"Yes, I see! Good show, you two."

"More friends of yours, I assume?" Great-grandfather asked. This was addressed to me, but Agnes thought he was talking to her.

"Mumble mumble brother," she replied—sullenly, of course.

Meantime, Maggot, looking over Tim's shoulder, was busy snickering in his high-pitched way. "Marines. Yeah. Heh, heh. Some Marine!"

Tim advanced threateningly on Great-grandfather and Bingo.

Agnes stepped in his path. "Tim, no. It's over. Let 'em go. The police will prob'ly be here any minute."

"Know what? I don't think so. I don't know how you got the old man here, but if he'd told anyone else, this place'd be crawlin' with cops already."

"Crawlin' wi' cops," echoed the snickering Maggot.

"STAND ASIDE," bellowed Augie, "you, you . . . "

"Brutish louts," I suggested.

" . . . you brutish louts!"

With that, Augie tried to march past Agnes and Tim and Maggot, holding Bingo on the far side away from them.

Tim grabbed Augie by the collar and practically lifted him off of his feet. Maggot pulled his knife and began twisting it in the air in a weird carving motion.

Agnes snatched Bingo away from Augie's good arm. She held him to her far side while reaching past Maggot to tug on Tim's sleeve. "No, Tim! No! He's an old man!"

"Aaaaaaa!" screamed the Twins. "Thursby what do we do?!"

"Stay with Bingo!" I cried from Augie's now hunched-up shoulder.

The girls ran around opposite sides of Tim's hat brim to the back. Without a moment's hesitation, they leapt from there to Maggot's shoulders—one on each side—and from there to Agnes, who held Bingo, who clung to Rumple. Rumple was being squeezed into the shape of an hour glass.

"Think it's that easy, do ya, Gramps?" sneered Tim. He shoved Augie back against peeling wallpaper and subjected him to a close-up view of a gummy sneer. "Think we're gonna run away like that tub a' lard Larry? Yeah, we seen 'im hoofin' it. Figured it took more than a scrawny geezer."

Nostrils flaring, yellow teeth chewing at the air, Maggot wheezed, "Lemme carve 'im, Tim! Lemme carve 'im like a jack o'lan'ern!"

Were Maggot someone for whom anyone might feel concern, one might have worried that he would faint from overexcitement. Maggot was not such a person.

"And that is fine with me, you miserable cretins," said Augie slowly and deliberately. "Because frankly, I don't think either of you would have the guts to really let me have it."

With that, Maggot gnashed his teeth and whined at a pitch quite like that of Dandie the Dandie Dinmont terrier after he's waited patiently for a bone but has had enough of waiting.

"Awright, Maggot, awright," began Tim, glaring at Augie, "but mebbe you should practice carving—" He spun around and finished with a mad cry—"ON A LITTLE ONE!"

★　　　★　　　★

46

First Mate Augustus versus The Louts, Part II

Tim's ferocious threat echoed in the little room. But Agnes and Bingo were not there.

Augie had seen something that I had missed in the terror of the moment—Agnes, carrying Bingo, had snuck out. The old fellow had challenged the louts, very possibly offering up his life, simply to buy time for Bingo to be carried to safety.

One after the other, Tim and Maggot gave chase. The air they left behind was positively blue with their obscenities. Their brand of obscenities, I should add, were far less imaginative than Augie's salty sailorisms referenced earlier.

Augie tried to follow, but he was even slower at going down stairs than up them.

"Slide, Augie!" I yelled. "Do you remember? The way you would speed down the bannister?"

"Right! Hold on!"

As a child, Augie had employed a sidesaddle, soaring-bird method for bannister sliding. As a septuagenarian, he used more of a lean-over-bannister, flailing-rag-doll style. Less graceful, to be sure, but soon enough we were on the landing outside.

Right away we saw Maggot sitting in our tilbury carriage. Poor Nellie strained against the reins, dragging the carriage forward and back as Maggot tried to hold her steady.

Nellie's struggle slowed Tim as he tried to force Agnes, with Bingo in her arms, up into the carriage.

Agnes, and Bingo, and the Twins for that matter, were screaming wildly. A garish display, but in keeping with the moment.

We lurched and bounced our way down the tenement's front steps.

"Stop those men!" cried Augie. "Stop them, I say!"

Not that anyone there could or would. Despite the early hour, in a better neighborhood the screams and shouts would have brought dozens of people into the street, all ready to help a woman with a baby in her arms. Not so in that forlorn corner of the Big City. The only hints at occupancy in the surrounding tenements were shutters shutting quickly.

As we have seen, though, a single brave soul can carry the day.

For example, my noble peace officer from the preceding night came at a full run once he heard the commotion. He rounded a corner still some distance down the street. His billy club was already at the ready. He blew the whistle held between his teeth with such force that it's a wonder he could breathe.

(Here the speaker engages in another gratuitous sound effect: a high-pitched whistle apparently emitted through his prominent front teeth.)

With that startling and unmistakeable sound, head-lout Tim quit trying to re-abduct Bingo. Casting Agnes and the boy out of his way, he climbed into the tilbury. Before Maggot could give the reins a shake, Tim shoved him out the other side of the carriage.

Maggot tumbled over the large, mud-encrusted wheels and onto the hard brick surface of the city street. He crumpled into a heap in the gutter.

"Hyah!" Tim yelled at Nellie, simultaneously cracking the whip at the old horse's back. Nellie had never felt such a cruel sting. The shock as much as the pain, I would think, caused her to bolt at full speed.

Augie and I arrived at street level, with the grimy heap of Maggot at our feet. Some movement from above and to one side caught my attention. Something the size of a small bird was swinging through the air like a pendulum—swinging right alongside Nellie as she fled.

From high above, I heard a proud chime ring out: "*Pa-ding!*"

Soaring at the end of the tugboat-winch rope, Pudding the mouse pulled alongside Nellie the horse.

At the appearance of a squeak-barking mouse at eye level, Nellie tilted her head and stared. I am reliably informed that neither head-tilting nor staring off to the side are typical for equines running at full gallop.

The identity-confused mouse continued to swing past the horse, ahead and upward, then back again like a returning pendulum right at Nellie's noble nose.

The stunned horse jerked her head back and stomped and skidded to a clattering stop.

The sudden halt catapulted Tim against the carriage dash and over it. He landed heavily on the street beside Nellie, but pulled himself up quickly.

Pudding had, in fact, collided with Nellie. Fortu-nately, horse noses are as soft as they are handsome, so neither creature was hurt. Pudding barked furiously at the brutish lout as she was air-lifted up and away.

In his fury, Tim didn't even notice the airborne, barking mouse. Instead he raised the whip, still clutched in his hand, to strike Nellie.

The officer's whistle sounded again just in time. Looking over his shoulder at the fast-approaching policeman, Tim dropped the whip and ran.

Augie stooped over the heap o' Maggot so briskly that I was thrown forward onto the red-brown bricks. Augie grabbed something out of Maggot's jacket. He straightened up quickly.

Something sharp and shiny launched from out of Augie's hand.

I spun around. Maggot's knife had already found its mark: Tim was pinned to a wooden doorjamb—through his jacket collar, that is.

He struggled free of his jacket, but it was too late: The police officer had him by the scruff of the neck.

"Learned that little trick on the Barbary coast," Augie explained as he lifted me back onto his shoulder.

We stepped around Maggot, who still looked like a shoe-smashed cockroach. Augie started to lurch toward the arresting officer. After a single lurch, or a lurch and a sway at most, Agnes started screaming again.

Maggot, clearly having faked his heapness, had sprung up for one last-ditch effort at surpassing his earlier stupidity. He was trying to wrest Bingo out of Agnes's arms. Perhaps he thought that he could somehow sneak away and renew the ransom request. To anyone with any sense, it was ridiculous. Of course, one does not study the criminal mind to learn about logic—only its absence.

"Gimme that brat!" Maggot shouted.

"Never!" cried Agnes.

"GIMME!" yelled Maggot again, jerking Bingo away forcefully. Maggot had force, but not control. Slipping from the sinister lout's hands, little Bingo was propelled up and away through the air.

Time seemed to stand still. I saw it, but I couldn't comprehend it. Bingo's own reaction, I think, added to the sense of unreality. Sailing through the ether on his back, the boy spotted the *Starry Night* above—too far away to help. "Birdie!" he giggled.

On each side of his diaper was a Twin—Gracie on the left and Ruby on the right. They clung to the cloth and desperately fluttered their little wings.

Still nestled against Bingo's chest, looking up at the distant airship as if watching clouds, Rumple applauded.

★   ★   ★

47

The Needed Stunner

One often reads, in tales of imaginary beings, about some last-minute revelation of magical powers. Unbeknownst even to the being who possesses them, the powers are usually held in reserve for climactic moments. The Twins' wings, sadly, held no such surprise. Bingo's trajectory left no doubt that the boy's arc would return him rapidly to Earth.

Fear not Ladies and Gentlemen! For the Flying Fays furnished the needed stunner—that climactic rescue required for the babe's survival, and for this story.

Loitering airborne nearby, the Flying Fays swooped in. It was as if they'd practiced for this moment a thousand times. First they left their usual formation. Then each Fay flew underneath Bingo at a different point under his body—one under his head, one between the shoulder blades, one under each arm, one at his lower back, and one under each leg. Bingo, of course, was no cloud, and continued to fall, but at a far more gentle pace.

"We're flying!" cried Gracie, not having noticed the Fays' arrival.

"We can fly!" cried Ruby.

The Fays, with some help from the Twins, certainly, lowered Bingo into Agnes's waiting arms.

"It's a miracle!" gasped Agnes. She stared at the child with a shocky look not unlike those we observed earlier in our visitors from the Matterhorn room. "It's like the good Lord set him down in my arms." She looked, wide-eyed, at Great-grandfather. "Do you suppose this means I'm forgiven? Could I be forgiven?"

Meanwhile the Twins were announcing their successful flight: "Did you see us, Thursby? We flew! We carried Bingo down from the sky!"

Here the Fays flew out from under Bingo and whirled into the sky like a tornado of little lights.

"Ahhh," sighed Gracie, "it was the Fays."

"Ahhh," sighed Ruby, "dag-nabbit."

"Don't be so sure," I said. "Your wings might've made all the difference."

The girls' enthusiasm returned immediately with a shared look of delight.

"Thursby's right!" piped Gracie. "Maybe it was the Fays *and* us!"

"Hooray for us!" crowed Ruby.

During this exchange with the Twins, Great-grandfather did not respond to Agnes's question about forgiveness. He appeared rather dazed and feeble. And as you may have noticed, I'm calling him *Great-grandfather* again. There is no skirting the truth: The exertion had caught up with him.

He was old again.

As Great-grandfather stared off into infinity, his lips parted. I thought he was about to speak, and I hoped it wouldn't be a comment to the Twins. Agnes and a belatedly gathering crowd would certainly think he was daft.

"Ack," he said simply from the good side of his mouth. His eyes rolled back, his head tilted. He began to pitch forward toward the hard brick street.

"AUGIE!" I yelled into his ear on our way down. He opened his eyes, but only in the instant before hitting the ground. I was able to jump and run before impact. Leaps from a moving Dinmont had trained me well.

In Great-grandfather's last-second glimpse, he saw below him not only the fast-approaching street, but also a translucent, baby-bluish, roundish figment.

Rumple had landed with Bingo into Agnes's arms. The Cozy had then climbed down to street level and started toddling toward us. I like to think that Rumple saw the glazed-over look on the old fellow's face. That maybe intuition inspired his actions.

However it came to pass, Rumple reached the right spot in the nick of time. What's more, when he saw Great-grandfather toppling toward him like a felled tree, Rumple opened his arms wide. Fearless, he was going to try to catch the old gent.

WHUMP! Oh, it hurt to see that frail old body crash, unsupported, against the grimy bricks of the city street. At least Rumple provided a soft, pillow-like landing for Great-grandfather's head.

Rumple, on the other hand, was fairly squished. Only his limbs and tapir-like proboscis extended from under the old fellow's wrinkled noggin.

By this time Gubbins and Musetta had descended from the airship. They joined us just as a human bystander rolled the collapsed septuagenarian over. Gubbins and I peeled Rumple off of Great-grandfather's face.

Rumple suffered only a temporary flattening. Plus there was an imprint of the old fellow's smooshed visage that wasn't a bad likeness. Unfazed, Rumple shook it off like a wet dog.

Gubbins, Musetta, and the Twins all stepped beside Rumple and me. Even the Flying Fays zipped back between the onlookers' legs, briefly landing on us and around us. Together we all looked upon Great-grandfather. He appeared to be unconscious.

Then he smacked his lips. And blinked his eyes. After several blinks, his eyes stayed open, the right more than the left. He glanced around at the humans who were peering down at him. Then his gaze fell sidelong upon the six of us, plus seven. He blinked again twice, but we were still there.

"I must be outta my gourd," he said.

*   *   *

48

Homecoming

Next exhibit, please.

(Flip-chart Exhibit #10: Untitled diagram showing points at which miniature flying beings might lower a small child.)

EXHIBIT #10

The seven Flying Fays, as it turned out, were Gubbins' first, and perhaps greatest, invention. On arriving at the country home after moving from the Big City, before even Great-grandfather was born, Gubbins had worried greatly about the nursery's location on the second floor. The alcove beckoned to children, then as now, as a snug play area. The window seat practically called out to small ones to climb up, stand on it, and to bounce. Only the windows and a latch stood between such children and the garden far below.

Gubbins retrieved seven volunteer sprites or pixies or what-have-you from the *Traumwelt*, and dipped them—humanely, no doubt—in liquified moonlight. He then trained each to its own special role. The Fays had only been needed for their intended purpose once: when they'd caught and lowered the catapulted Bingo outside the louts' lair in the Big City. Once, I'm sure you'll agree, is enough.

Now that I have alluded to liquified moonlight, you might ask why we don't use that powerful concoction more often. Suffice it to say that Gubbins had discovered the dangers of the stuff while inventing it. But that, Ladies and Gentlemen, is a tale for another time.

We arrived home in Father's carriage with Nellie following by a tether. The tilbury had been given on the spot to our police officer. As the officer would tell reporters, technically he had already gone off duty. The suspicious behavior of Agnes and Larry, though, had vexed him all through the night. The good officer had decided to make one last, early morning pass by the louts' tenement. Upon hearing the hullabaloo he'd come running.

That same night, Bridie had wasted no time in sharing the story of Athair Críonna's dream-inspired knowledge. By the time we rolled up the front drive, servants, neighbors, reporters, and other well-wishers lined the driveway, gazing upon the old fellow like a returning prophet.

For his part, Great-grandfather wisely declined to speak further about his revelatory dream. Nor would he discuss the elegant, rabbit-headed messenger.

Bingo's homecoming was otherwise as you would expect—emotional, gleeful, and a relief. Mother sobbed so heavily that Bridie whisked her off to bed again. Father broke down in tears of joy.

Bingo proved a resilient little soldier. Now that he was back with his mama and papa, he seemed little worse for the wear. For days after his return, though, he would hardly let Rumple out of his sight. And he would always fall asleep best when Rumple was near.

This continued even after Bingo became a boy called Ben, who could no longer see Rumple until he closed his eyes and drifted off to that mystical world of clouds and stars and imagination.

⭑   ⭑   ⭑

49

Second Chances

Before we wrap up for the day, you may be curious as to what happened to some of the other personalities in this tale.

As to the brutish lout and the sinister lout—Agnes's brother, Tim, that is, and his cohort Dave, alias Maggot—no surprises there. Both spent many, many years in prison. Hopefully they shared the same cell together—poetic justice, *n'est-ce pas?*

Their less-loutish accomplice, Larry, was never heard from again. One likes to think that he learned his lesson, counted himself lucky, and turned away from a life of crime.

Agnes initially went to jail for her involvement in the caper. Her husband, Orville, stood by his *Aggie* even when things looked dark for her. At the inquiry, though, it was determined that Agnes had truly believed that her evil brother would harm Bingo if she did not "play ball." In other words, as the magistrate put it, Agnes had only cooperated "under duress." That is not to say that she made good decisions, of course. Still, as Great-grandfather pointed out, the one-time nanny had helped to get Bingo out of the hideout at a crucial moment. She also testified against the louts. For these reasons, Agnes eventually received a pardon.

Through later newspaper reports and conversations in the drawing room, we learned more about Agnes's story. Once released from jail, she returned to her husband. Although they could not have children of their own, they knew that many children needed loving parents. Both Orville and Agnes, in fact, had been orphans themselves.

Hesitant, even scared, the two went to the boys' orphanage where Orville had spent much of his childhood.

"I can't do it," said Agnes, stopping at the gate.

"We'll just visit this one time," promised Orville.

The staff at the orphanage let them watch the children in the play yard. In an area set aside for the younger children, Agnes found her gaze returning to a tiny fellow, maybe two years old. His hair was black, not blond. His eyes were dark, not pale. Yet Agnes saw something like her babkins in the boy. Something that tugged at her heart.

Before she knew it, Agnes found that she had stepped nearer to the play area. The tiny boy saw that he was being watched. He stood and looked at Agnes in return. After a few minutes, the lad dusted off the breeches of his little uniform, and inched closer.

For a moment he stood still, staring up at Agnes with large brown eyes. Agnes and the boy simply looked at each other.

"Mumble mumble mumbly?" asked the boy in a voice as wee as he.

"What's that?" asked Agnes, leaning forward.

The boy looked down, afraid. When he looked up at her again, he raised his voice just enough to be heard.

"Will you be my mommy?"

Agnes straightened up and clapped one hand over her mouth. Her eyes welled with tears as she looked at her husband. Orville gave a quick nod.

Aggie bent over and scooped the child into her arms.

"I will!" she promised. "Forever and always!"

★   ★   ★

50

Athair Crionna Says Goodnight

Now let us return closer in time to the night of Bingo's rescue—specifically, to about two weeks afterward. Agnes still sat in jail. Mother still spent much time in bed, but people did not seem as worried about her as before. After the experiment with Nellie, Pudding had found her inner dog, which turned out to be a border collie. She tried to find creatures to corral at every opportunity.

And Great-grandfather . . . he was not fairing well. The science of figmentology, however, helps to explain how the old fellow could see me and other figments without the help of moonlight. Our visibility told us much about his placement between this world and the next.

Small children can see Cozies because they do not yet distinguish between the so-called real world and the world of dreams. The same thing is true at the other end of the line. When humans reach the point when they are almost ready to cross over to the afterlife, they sometimes spend their last days with one foot in the world of dreams. This provides a kind of stepping stone for the soul.

Great-grandfather had likely neared that point when I approached him for help on the night of Bingo's rescue. Theoretically speaking, seeing me in the moonlight might have opened up his mind's eye to the in-between realm. One could say that Great-grandfather was about to go through a doorway into a garden. He already had his hand on the doorknob, but the glass panes in the door were covered. The moonlight had simply pushed the curtains aside for him to see through.

As I was saying, a couple weeks after our adventure, I was visiting my old boy again as he rested in his four-poster bed. I'd been spending quite a bit of time with him there. Sometimes he spotted me, other times not. This time, there was no doubt.

"Hello, old friend," he said softly, glancing over at me on the pillow beside him. "Or maybe, 'Goodbye,' hm?"

I smoothed my ears and straightened my jacket. Although we Cozies know that such partings are only temporary, they are always difficult. "Neither," I said. "Let's say, '*Auf Wiedersehen.*' For I promise you, my boy, we will meet again."

"Yes?" he asked. "I'm glad. Take care of Bingo."

"We will."

"G'night."

"Good night, Augie."

With that, I gave him a kiss on the forehead. Then I lay back down on the pillow for a bit, pondering what a strange and mysterious thing is life.

⋆　　⋆　　⋆

51

Stork!

(The speaker turns away from the audience for a moment to compose himself. After a moment, he returns his royal-blue handkerchief to his coat pocket and continues.)

We Cozies did our best to get back to into a routine. Ah, routines. How blesséd they seem, after danger has disrupted monotony!

Our return to routine, however, would not last. A new, joyful adventure was about to begin.

'Twas again the first Tuesday of the month, the night planned for Musetta's oft-postponed performance of *Pining Maiden, Part III*. We had found our places on the window-seat cushions and the big burgundy pillow.

Our theatrical performances, of course, were usually scheduled for mid-afternoon. Rather than risk another interruption, we had decided to wait. Since morning the humans in the household had seemed awfully agitated.

Even the new nanny had kept going out into the hall, whispering to other humans, and returning. The new nanny was, by the by, a softish, round young woman, hardly more than a girl herself. She also happened to be the niece of our own Bridie.

A man with a black bag and a lady assistant had come to visit Mother in her room. They were still in there, for all we knew. Father had been downstairs in the drawing room most of the day, pacing.

By evening, the household seemed to settle down. With Dandie resting nearby, Bridie's niece rocked Bingo in his crib. The Moon was in the sky outside the nursery windows. This provided a very different, but still effective backdrop.

Musetta—billed now as *Brave Musetta, Champion of Operation Moonlight*—took the stage. She lifted the back of one hand to the amethyst broach at her forehead. She closed her eyes.

And . . . a baby's cry rang out—*loudly!* We all jumped up and turned, but it was not Bingo. The noise came from down the hall.

Musetta slouched with the back of one wrist against her hip. "Gee, an interruption. Who'd've guessed!"

"It's a girl! *Begorrah*, it's a baby girl!" shouted Bridie as she ran from Mother's room and down the stairs.

Gracie scrunched up her face. "A new baby?!"

"Where do you suppose *that* came from?" Ruby asked, lifting her arms in a palms-up shrug.

Musetta and I looked at each other and explained, in unison, "Stork!"

Rumple ran up the big burgundy pillow to the window sill. The alleged delivery bird had already vanished. But the Moon, framed by a misty halo in the night sky, beamed a great smile and gave us all a reassuring wink.

> (The speaker steps away from the podium and bows his head to signal the end of today's talk.)

★   ★   ★

EPILOGUE

Question and Answer Session

Thank you, Ladies and Gentlemen. Thank you. You are too kind.

(Pause for applause to die down.)

If there are any questions, I believe we have a few minutes left.

Question #1: So, are you saying that imagination is important because, if you have a bunch of imaginary beings running around your house and your kid ends up kidnapped, they might be able to help, if the moon happens to be out?

(The speaker sighs.)

Answer #1: Not exactly, sir. My lecture is meant more allegorically. Take Pudding, for example. She imagined herself to be a dog, and by the strength of her imagination, she achieved what a dog might do—rounding up Nellie at a crucial moment.

Question #2: Uh, no offense, Thursby, sir, but, an imaginary rabbit? Hasn't the anthropomorphized rabbit been done to death? I mean, Lewis Carroll, Beatrix Potter . . .

Answer #2: Ah, yes. Thank you for the opportunity of addressing that issue. First, as I've said, I am a figment with *features* of an English lop—most notably head, fur, and feet—and not a rabbit outright. Second, young Augie dreamt me up long before most of the popular rabbit-related fiction of which you speak. Finally, it is my opinion that lagomorph popularity stems from the natural adorableness of the species. Therefore I ask you, please, don't hate us because we're beautiful.

Question #3: Would you teach me how to tie a cravat?

(The speaker pushes one ear back and lifts his head slightly to better display his own neckcloth.)

Answer #3: I would be delighted! Please see me after. Also, copies of the classic *Neckclothitania* are available from my publisher at a reasonable price.

Question #4: Would you pop out of a cake at my child's birthday party?

Answer #4: Next question.

Question #5: Are you in love with Musetta?

Answer #5: I'm afraid we're out of time. Thank you all for coming.

The End

About the Author

T.L. FISCHER holds a Bachelor of Arts degree in English Literature from McGill University of Montreal, Canada, as well as two advanced degrees in far less interesting subjects. While pursuing his education, Fischer studied in both France and England.

A long time ago, Fischer worked as a technical writer, as an editor of online software documentation, and as a freelance writer. Then for many years he worked professionally with victims of family violence and violence against children. These latter experiences led Fischer to write about the Cozies and their world of simple pleasures, where imagination protects the innocent.

Fischer and his spouse, D, are avid dog lovers. D volunteers for animal welfare causes while Fischer writes.

Visit *tlfischer.net* to read more about the diverse writings of T.L. Fischer.

COMING SOON

Moon Song

by T.L. Fischer

An old-fashioned,
rhyming adventure
for the very young
(and young at heart.)